High
School
Prodigies
Have It
Easy
Even in
Another
World!

8

©Sacraneco

"We meet again, Tsukasa."

**When her eyes came into view,
Tsukasa saw that they glowed with
*the same light they had once before.***

©Sacraneco

Not a single one of the soldiers saw this coming. A shocked stir ran through the crowd.

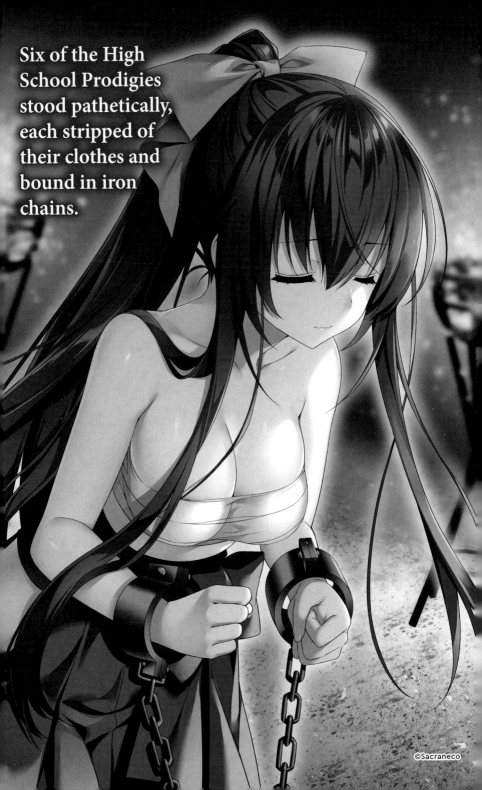

Six of the High School Prodigies stood pathetically, each stripped of their clothes and bound in iron chains.

©Sacraneco

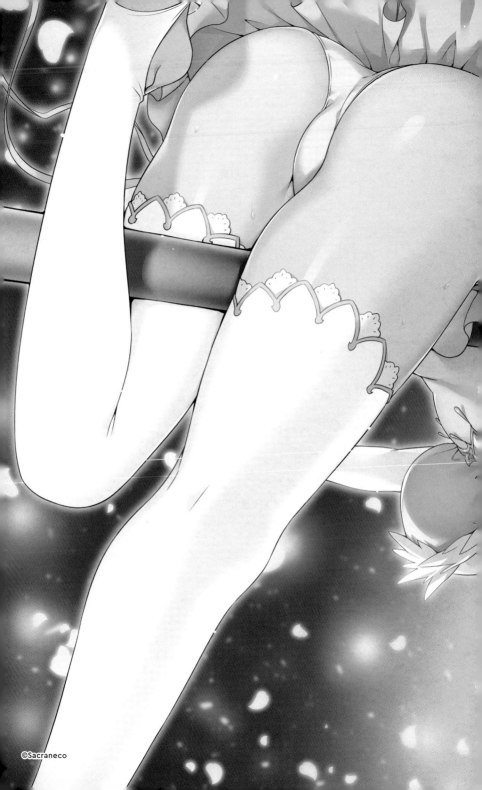

©Sacraneco

I gotta make sure I really get things **popping** in here.

Shinobu's risqué dance got the audience fired up like never before.

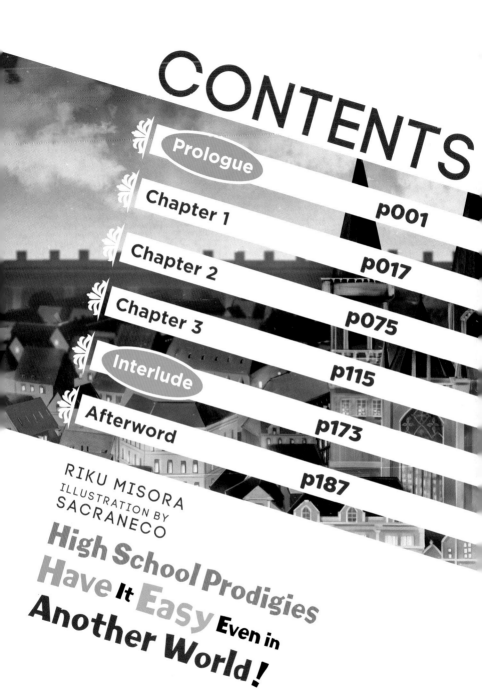

CONTENTS

RIKU MISORA
ILLUSTRATION BY
SACRANECO

High School Prodigies Have It Easy Even in Another World!

©Sacraneco

High School Prodigies Have It Easy Even in Another World!

8

Riku Misora

Illustration by SACRANECO

YEN
ON
NEW YORK

High School Prodigies Have It Easy Even in Another World! 8

Riku Misora

TRANSLATION BY NATHANIEL HIROSHI THRASHER
COVER ART BY SACRANECO

This book is a work of fiction. Names, characters, places, and incidents are the product of the author's imagination or are used fictitiously. Any resemblance to actual events, locales, or persons, living or dead, is coincidental.

CHOUJIN KOUKOUSEI TACHI HA ISEKAI DEMO YOYU DE IKINUKU YOUDESU! Vol. 8
Copyright © 2019 Riku Misora
Illustrations copyright © 2019 Sacraneco
First published in Japan in 2019 by SB Creative, Tokyo.
English translation rights arranged with SB Creative, Tokyo through TUTTLE-MORI AGENCY, INC., Tokyo

English translation © 2023 by Yen Press, LLC

Yen Press, LLC supports the right to free expression and the value of copyright. The purpose of copyright is to encourage writers and artists to produce the creative works that enrich our culture.

The scanning, uploading, and distribution of this book without permission is a theft of the author's intellectual property. If you would like permission to use material from the book (other than for review purposes), please contact the publisher. Thank you for your support of the author's rights.

Yen On
150 West 30th Street, 19th Floor
New York, NY 10001

Visit us at yenpress.com
facebook.com/yenpress ★ twitter.com/yenpress
yenpress.tumblr.com ★ instagram.com/yenpress

First Yen On Edition: May 2023
Edited by Yen On Editorial: Jordan Blanco
Designed by Yen Press Design: Liz Parlett

Yen On is an imprint of Yen Press, LLC.
The Yen On name and logo are trademarks of Yen Press, LLC.

The publisher is not responsible for websites (or their content) that are not owned by the publisher.

Library of Congress Cataloging-in-Publication Data
Names: Misora, Riku, author. | Sacraneco, illustrator. | Thrasher, Nathaniel Hiroshi, translator.
Title: High school prodigies have it easy even in another world! / Riku Misora ;
illustration by Sacraneco ; translation by Nathaniel Hiroshi Thrasher.
Other titles: Chōjin-Kokoseitachi wa Isekai demo Yoyu de Ikinuku Yodesu! English
Identifiers: LCCN 2020016894 | ISBN 9781975309725 (v. 1 ; trade paperback) |
ISBN 9781975309749 (v. 2 ; trade paperback) | ISBN 9781975309763 (v. 3 ; trade paperback) |
ISBN 9781975309787 (v. 4 ; trade paperback) | ISBN 9781975309800 (v. 5 ; trade paperback) |
ISBN 9781975309824 (v. 6 ; trade paperback) | ISBN 9781975350086 (v. 7 ; trade paperback) |
ISBN 9781975350109 (v. 8 ; trade paperback)
Subjects: CYAC: Fantasy. | Gifted persons—Fiction. | Imaginary places—Fiction | Magic—Fiction.
Classification: LCC PZ7.M6843377 Hi 2020 | DDC [Fic]—dc23
LC record available at https://lccn.loc.gov/2020016894

ISBNs: 978-1-9753-5010-9 (paperback)
978-1-9753-5011-6 (ebook)

10 9 8 7 6 5 4 3 2 1

LSC-C

Printed in the United States of America

PROLOGUE

⚜ Adel's Notes ⚜

Thanks in no small part to the High School Prodigies' intervention, the battle between Mayoi's self-governing dominion and Kaguya's rebel forces ended in the latter's victory.

Upon being freed from Mayoi's spell, the people of Yamato returned to themselves, furious at how the Freyjagard Empire had violated their dignity.

However, that triumph came at a heavy price. Mayoi had brainwashed her side into mindlessly charging at their foes, and as a result, both sides suffered tremendous losses. Upon the war's conclusion, the whole of Yamato echoed with the hellish groans and cries of rage from the wounded.

One of the Prodigies, Keine Kanzaki, quickly took charge of the relief effort. In addition to barking orders at all the Yamato physicians, she used her own skills to treat her way through the casualties. Thanks to her efforts, all those in need of urgent care were tended to in five days.

On the evening of the fifth day, she announced at the improvised infirmary set up in the town hall that it was safe to disband the emergency medical corps.

As soon as she did, the physicians working nonstop day and night lay down where they stood and slept like the dead. Not even Keine was immune to the ravages of exhaustion, and she also dozed off peacefully in her chair.

Lyrule, who'd been using her magic to assist Keine as she had back in the Gustav domain, went around draping quilts over the collapsed staffers.

"Whew."

After hanging the final quilt over Keine's shoulders, she sighed lightly. Her responsibilities had been far less stressful than the medics', but she hadn't been able to relax since Mayoi and Jade had attacked her and the Prodigies back at Azuchi Castle. Going through something like that was enough to exhaust anyone mentally and physically. Lyrule wished to curl up and pass out as much as everyone else.

However, she refrained from doing so.

After doling out quilts, she exited through the back. Then...

"Hnn!"

...she gave herself a light clap on the cheeks.

Drowsiness was clouding her mind, and she couldn't have that. There was something she had to do, and now was the time for it.

Lyrule sat down against the pile of wooden crates behind the town hall and withdrew an aged journal from her pocket.

"This belonged to Adel..."

Adel was a merchant who'd died in Yamato making good on his obligation to its people. He was Elch's father, and Lyrule thought of him as hers, too. Adel had taken Lyrule in after discovering her abandoned in the forest. It was because of his teachings that she was literate, despite being raised in a mountain village.

This journal's original owner was very important to Lyrule.

Plus, Tsukasa had told her something after he'd read the diary.

"There's some information in this journal that concerns you specifically."

Had Adel written a message for her?

Had he left Lyrule a note as he died alone in a foreign land?

If so, she wanted to read it.

She *needed* to read it.

Lyrule had been busy since arriving in Yamato as an Elm ambassador. She'd been pursued, caught in a huge battle, and, until moments ago, occupied with the aftermath of that conflict. That wasn't to say there'd been no chances to sit down and read the journal, but with so many responsibilities, she'd lacked the emotional energy to confront Adel's death.

Now that things were at a lull, her mind was settled.

Lyrule could spend time reading of Adel's death without worrying about anything else.

And so...

"Here we go."

...she opened the journal and began tracing the path of her surrogate father's life.

The contents were just as Tsukasa had described. Entries detailed Adel's daily activities, thoughts about his food, transaction records, and sketches of things he spotted on his travels. From the look of it, Adel used the journal less as a formal account for his job and more as an idle time-killing method on the road, something to jog his memory later when he wanted to regale Winona with stories of his travels. The sketch-laden writings painted vivid pictures of the people, locations, and cuisine Adel had encountered during his trips to distant lands. Lyrule found herself engrossed, unable to stop reading. Before she knew it, her drowsiness was blown away to a foreign country of its own.

"...!"

However, all the writing's wonder and delight were abruptly replaced with panic.

When Adel ventured to Yamato to forge inroads to new markets, he got lost in a deep forest. His supplies ran dry swiftly, he was attacked by poisonous snakes, and he had to hide for fear of drawing the attention of predators...

Reading from one entry to the next was like watching Adel wither away in real time, and each dedicated more and more length to the man's love for Winona.

It tore at Lyrule's heart, but she still couldn't stop.

She knew that salvation lay a few pages beyond, after all.

Earlier, Tsukasa had explained that after Adel got lost in the forest, he was saved by a village of elves. After getting to know the villagers, he made connections there that allowed him to introduce Yamato's then-emperor, Gekkou, to an elf woman named Hinowa, and the pair were later married. As their matchmaker, Adel earned the nation's unwavering trust, and his quest to open the Yamato markets was successful.

Sure enough, that was precisely how it occurred in the writing.

Adel's market trailblazing led to enormous profits for the Orion Company—his affiliate. The journal was filled with Adel's gratitude for the elves and the Yamato people. There was no reason to think his words were untruthful, especially not after how he'd elected to throw in his fate with theirs. When the Freyjagard Empire brought its overwhelming menace to bear against Yamato, Adel stood with his friends and allies until his final moments.

"..."

When Lyrule remembered how Adel had died, her hand hesitated to take the next page. For turning it would begin the story of Adel's demise.

Lyrule wasn't about to turn back now, though.

Her adopted father had treated her as his own, and she loved him dearly. If he left some kind of message for her, she needed to read it.

After steeling her resolve, Lyrule turned the page...

Today, I was asked to adopt an elf baby.

...and went stiff.

Today, I was asked to adopt an elf baby.

I hadn't returned to the elf village in ages, and when I visited, the village head couple made a request of me.

I owe them my life for accepting me into the village after Hinowa rescued me, and when I opened trade with Yamato, I had friendly negotiations with the two village leaders on more than one occasion. They're good, honorable people, and I know better than anyone that they wouldn't give up their child without good reason. So when they asked me, I wasn't surprised or horrified.

Naturally, I did ask why they were doing this. Their reply was:

"The evil dragon is working to be reborn."

The elves practice a religion called the Seven Luminaries, and the evil dragon is the enemy of their god, Yggdra. More than a thousand years ago, it invaded from another world and laid waste to civilization. But Yggdra and seven brave heroes she called in from a different realm were able to seal the menace within a cycle of rebirth. Then

Yggdra transformed into a massive tree. She set down her roots to restore the war-ravaged land and passed along the teachings of the Seven Luminaries.

The Yggdra tree exists to this day somewhere deep in the village. Only the village heads are permitted to enter the sanctum, and yesterday, they told me that Yggdra issued an ominous prophecy. Apparently, the evil dragon has resurrected its followers and plots to have them destroy the seal so that it may descend upon us again.

According to the village-leader couple, one of their ancestors fought alongside Yggdra as her follower way back when. Ever since, a descendant of each generation has carried the seal within their soul, passing it from parent to child.

In other words, the seal rests within the baby.

Soon, the evil dragon's followers will come after the child as part of their scheme to revive the dragon. Tearing her soul to shreds will undo the lock.

That's why they need me to keep the baby hidden—to safeguard the world and the child.

Once I take the baby, they plan to abandon the village and travel with their kin to the New World south across the sea. They hope to draw the evil dragon's followers' attention away from the child. We don't even have safe shipping routes across the southern ocean yet, and they know that one way or another, it's a one-way journey.

I'm thrilled and honored they trust me enough to leave their beloved daughter in my care. To be honest, though, I'm having trouble accepting everything they've told me. It's hard to see Yggdra and the evil dragon as anything more than fairy tales. They believe in those myths so strongly, they're willing to relinquish their child and embark on a nearly suicidal journey... I'd be lying if I claimed it didn't give me pause.

But at the same time...I know full well how important the elves of this village consider the teachings of the Seven Luminaries to be, and I also know how much they revere Yggdra. Their gratitude and fidelity have survived for more than a millennium, and piety like that should be held sacred. It would be the height of conceit to impose my values on them.

And so…I agreed to their request.

My son, Elch, was born not too long ago, and I promised the two village leaders that I'd show their daughter the same amount of love and that I'd raise her into a kind, upstanding adult.

For the rest of my days, I'll never forget the looks on their faces.

Their lips were pursed tight, like they were fighting back a pain that threatened to tear them in half. Yet they thanked me for accepting their request all the same. They knew this was best for their child.

I'll never be able to share with her just how much they loved her or the tears they shed that day. Her parents requested I tell her nothing of the elves. They wish for her to grow up as an ordinary girl.

They don't want to leave her with such a heavy burden.

All they hope is for her to live a happy life.

I asked them for one thing: the child's name.

I wanted to share their love with her, even if that was the only way I could.

At my question, the village leaders' pained expressions turned to weak smiles, like they'd found salvation, and they spoke the name of their beloved daughter.

The word means a blessing from God in the language of the civilization the evil dragon destroyed.

Lyrule.

The girl's name is Lyrule. She's the daughter of my dear friends, and as of today, she's a member of my family.

7

"…"

Lyrule stared in shock at the writing.

The story behind her birth was laid out, plain as day. It all happened so fast that Lyrule couldn't process the information for a moment. Her mind was at a standstill.

The stiffness spread to her hands, and the journal tumbled from between her fingers.

"Ah…"

She stooped to pick it up. The moment she did, the moonlight illuminating her was blotted out by a shadow.

When Lyrule looked up…

"H-hello…Tsukasa."

…she saw a heterochromatic young man standing there. Lyrule knew this boy.

"I came to speak with Keine about something, but I thought I saw you collapse," he replied.

Tsukasa had come running over after misreading the situation. He gave Lyrule an awkward smile. "Judging by the state you're in, I take it you read the journal."

"I did." Lyrule nodded and stood with the book in hand. "So when Adel said I was abandoned, that was a lie."

"It would appear so."

"To be honest…the possibility had already crossed my mind."

"Had it?"

Lyrule bobbed her head.

The contents of Adel's journal were a shock, to be sure. However, it wasn't the kind of surprise that accompanied something wild and unexpected. It was the sort that followed a hunch Lyrule had carried for a long while.

Tsukasa and the other Prodigies had appeared in this world conspicuously close to Lyrule.

Her origins were unknown, but she looked like the people whose folklore seemed connected to the Prodigies' arrival.

That strange voice had spoken to her.

And finally…Adel, the man who had found Lyrule, had a close connection with the elves she so resembled.

There was no way all of that was a mere coincidence.

"Adel and Ulgar were the ones who supposedly found me. It was probably easy for Adel to make it appear like he'd come upon me in the forest alone."

"True enough. He likely hid you in the forest ahead of time, then took the village mayor with him to go 'discover' you. That way, his story about you being an abandoned child would seem more believable."

"I wonder if he kept the story about my origins a secret from Winona, too?"

"I imagine he did, yes," Tsukasa said. "She never acted like she harbored a secret. Based on the journal entries, I think Adel did everything in his power to make good on his saviors' request to raise you as a normal girl. My guess is he believed Winona would show you as much love as she did her child, even without knowing the full context."

"I…I see."

Lyrule knew how sincere a person Adel was. Considering that the request had come from people who'd saved his life, she had little doubt that he would have done whatever he could to honor it.

Noticing Lyrule's downcast expression, Tsukasa posed her a question. "Are you upset that he kept the truth from you?"

However…

"No."

…Lyrule gave her head a determined shake.

She *was* a little curious about whether or not Winona knew the story, but no matter the answer, it wouldn't change that their love was real. Lyrule was confident of that. If anything, Lyrule's being a girl might have led Winona to take even better care of her than she had Elch.

And Lyrule felt the same way about Adel, too. He'd lied only to protect her. She could hardly blame him for that.

She had a pair of biological parents who birthed and protected her and another pair who raised her, and all wished for her happiness.

Thanks to their efforts, she grew up healthy and strong.

"I thought I was an abandoned baby, but…the truth is, there are so, so many people who care about me."

It was an incredibly happy thought.

But at the same time…

"However, learning what they spent so much effort to keep hidden is… It's a little scary." Lyrule clutched her shoulders.

According to Adel's journal, a huge tree deep within the elf village was seen as the literal incarnation of Yggdra, god of the Seven Luminaries. Talk of deities was typically written off as fable, but the Seven Heroes really existed, brought from some other world. And Lyrule had confirmed the existence of an entity that made contact with her to guide them.

Was the entity truly a god? Or was it just pretending to be one, like the Prodigies?

Lyrule didn't know, but there was definitely *something* paranormal waiting for them.

Once they met with it, they would finally learn the evil dragon's nature and get answers to the many other questions that had piled up. That would make it easier for Tsukasa and the others to determine their course of action. But at the same time, a conversation with Yggdra would likely reveal things that could spell the end for Lyrule's chance at a normal life. No, actually…

…*it's more than just a chance.*

Lyrule was certain.

Everything that had happened to her and everything she'd read in Adel's journal hinted that she possessed a special role to play in the coming major events. It was frightening. Learning one's existence was tied to the fate of the world was enough for anyone to feel lost and afraid.

However…

"I'd still like you to accompany us to the elf village, though."

…even after hearing of her worries, Tsukasa asked Lyrule to join them.

"The evil dragon's true nature is an essential piece of information, both for the world at large and for our own desire to learn if Neuro is trustworthy after he tried to keep the entity's existence a secret.

"Yggdra, god of the Seven Luminaries, definitely has the answer. Both times she contacted us, it was through using you as an intermediary. I think it's safe to assume that you need to be present for us to interact with her.

"I do appreciate your worry regarding the seal mentioned in the journal, the evil dragon's followers trying to break it, and about life changing in huge, irreversible ways. However…I hope you're still willing to fight through those fears and lend us your strength."

Tsukasa offered no empty words of comfort or thoughtless

encouragement. All he gave Lyrule were honest words and his determined gaze.

Upon hearing his voice and seeing his expression...

I'm such an idiot...

...Lyrule was overcome with regret.

If she wasn't there, there was a good chance they wouldn't be able to communicate with the presumably Yggdra entity who had spoken through Lyrule previously. They'd even discussed that issue on their way to Yamato. Yet, after all that, she was cowering in fear and hoping for sympathy. What was she *doing*?

Lyrule could whine all she liked, but Tsukasa's reply was always going to be the same: "I know it's a lot to ask, but please try to hang in there." That was all he *could* say. The information they stood to gain from this meeting was essential, both for the world and the Prodigies. As the team's leader, Tsukasa bore the weight of the hard decisions. His position didn't allow him to indulge Lyrule's hesitation, and he wasn't the kind of person to compromise on his responsibilities. However, he wasn't the sort to shrug off a necessary evil when others had to make sacrifices. On the contrary, Tsukasa accepted all the grudges and resentment and anguished over them more than those angry with him.

And Lyrule already knew all that. It was the whole reason she'd fallen in love with him.

Tsukasa was willing to sacrifice anything for the sake of others, and she wished dearly to be a shoulder for him to lean on.

But here I am...

Lyrule was bemoaning something Tsukasa had no power to fix and hurting him for no good reason.

Her brow furrowed in pained regret.

And in her heart...that regret turned to resolve.

She held Adel's journal close to her chest. "Of course. I'll be there."

"I'm sorry about this; I really am. I know that having you learn more about the Seven Luminaries goes directly against the wish your parents made when they gave you to Adel, but..."

"Please don't worry about it. Look..." When Tsukasa tried to apologize, Lyrule twirled her body like a dancer. After displaying herself in all her splendor, she added, "I'm not a child anymore.

"My mother gave birth to me, and my father entrusted me to Adel, who accepted me into his family, and Winona raised me.

"So many people showed me love and helped me grow into the person I am.

"Now it's on me to become an adult worthy of all that care."

Lyrule wasn't a child who needed sheltering anymore. She was an adult who could protect others the way many did for her—even if that wasn't what her parents wished for her.

All children had to leave the nest someday.

"And if I can do that by helping the people I care about, then all the better."

No trepidation remained on Lyrule's face.

Tsukasa's expression softened a little...

"I'm glad to hear that. I really appreciate it. The plan is to set out tomorrow at noon, and it's going to be a long day, so make sure to get your rest."

...then he told Lyrule about the plans to leave Azuchi and departed in the direction of the town hall.

He needed to go tell Keine the same thing.

As Lyrule watched him go, a thought crossed her mind.

She hadn't lied when she expressed a desire to aid the people dear to her...

©Sacraneco

…but it would have been more accurate to say the *person* she cared about.

Oh gosh.

Lyrule couldn't help but laugh at herself a little. She had to feel better if she could come up with such bold thoughts.

CHAPTER 1

⚜ The Final Piece ⚜

The self-governing dominion had previously seized prodigy inventor Ringo Oohoshi's off-road truck, but the High School Prodigies had it back now, and their group loaded into it and left Yamato's capital, Azuchi, in search of the Seven Luminaries' origin and the elf village with deep ties to it.

The truck's passengers included all the High School Prodigies, except Masato Sanada, and Yamato's new samurai general, Shura, who traveled with them as a bodyguard.

The order for her to go along had come from Yamato's new empress, Kaguya. Yamato owed the High School Prodigies a debt for helping liberate the country, so Kaguya insisted they be kept safe. However, that was only a pretense. Kaguya couldn't come because she and her war council were busy preparing for the battle to maintain sovereignty, so she wanted Shura to go in her stead to investigate why the Prodigies had come to this world and the evil dragon's identity.

Tsukasa had already told Kaguya and Shura that he and the other Prodigies weren't angels but humans who'd been summoned from another world by an unknown entity. Kaguya and Shura had every right to that knowledge, considering the huge number of lives they were responsible for and the potential threat. Plus, the Prodigies had no particular reason to hide anything from them. They welcomed Shura with open arms and headed for the elf village together.

On their way there...

"Urrrrrgh..."

...one of the High School Prodigies, the magician Prince Akatsuki, groaned.

Shinobu Sarutobi gave him a concerned look. "What's wrong, Akatsuki? Feeling carsick?"

"Well, there's that, too," Akatsuki said, looking decidedly pale. "But I mostly just haven't been able to sleep. When I try, all the stuff I saw in the war keeps flashing through my head..."

The clash between Mayoi's dominion army and Kaguya's resistance forces had concluded only several days ago. Akatsuki had seen a lot he wished he could forget when he'd stood on the front lines.

People were cut down by katanas, while others were beaten to death by clubs. Akatsuki saw warriors pulverized under the weight of others charging over them.

He never had to think about anything so horrific in his peaceful life in Japan. Akatsuki was still a sensitive teenager, and seeing those horrors left heavy wounds on his psyche that drove him to exhaustion.

Between that and the carsickness, his body was reaching its breaking point.

"Are you all right? I'd be happy to prescribe you some anti-anxiety meds or something to help you sleep," Keine Kanzaki offered from the seat behind Akatsuki's.

"Thanks, but no thanks. If I slept, I'd just end up having nightmares…"

"That's rough, buddy," Shinobu said.

"Oh yeah, actually, that reminds me. Shinobu, what the hell?!"

"Huh? Little ol' me? What'd I do?"

Shinobu gave her head an adorable tilt to the side as though to say, "Who, me?"

"You seriously forgot?!" Akatsuki shouted indignantly. "You gave me those pills and were like, *'My family's passed down the secret recipe for these steelskin pills for generations. They'll make your skin hard enough to repel arrows.'* And it was all a load of bull! You had me scared out of my mind!"

Akatsuki had been shaking in his boots right before he and Shinobu joined up with Tsukasa and the rebel army for the assault on Azuchi Castle. So Shinobu had fed him a story to get him motivated to fight. Akatsuki had believed her to the point of standing in the line of fire, an act that proved deeply harrowing. When Akatsuki thought back on it, he grew furious with the Prodigy journalist.

Unfortunately, Akatsuki was so ridiculously adorable that he didn't come across as scary in the slightest, and as a result, Shinobu was entirely unrepentant. "Oho, you wound me. I wasn't lying, you know—that *is* what my family told me when they taught me the recipe. I mean, I've never actually tried them, but still."

"Maybe you could've mentioned that before you talked them up! Ugh, just remembering it is making me scared…"

"Nya-ha-ha. Sorry, sorry. To make it up to you, starting tonight, I'll sleep with you until you're tired enough to snooze like a baby. ♪"

"What?! Hey, g-g-g-g-g-girls shouldn't say stuff like that!"

"Hmmmm? *'Stuff like that'*? I was just talking about lying

in bed together and reading aloud until you dozed off. What did youuuu think I was talking about?"

"~~~~~~!"

Shinobu smirked, grinning as smugly as the Cheshire Cat.

When Akatsuki realized she was messing with him, he teared up and cried to Tsukasa, who was sitting in the seat ahead of the magician's. "Wahhh! Tsukasaaaa, Shinobu's being a bully!"

"Shinobu, don't poke fun at Akatsuki. Unlike Merchant, he's not used to that kind of teasing."

Shinobu stuck her tongue out a little at Tsukasa's admonishment. "Fiiiine." Not a moment later, she said, "Buuut," and her impish smile returned. "If you do wanna do 'stuff like that,' Akatsuki, then I'd be down. You were pretty cool back there. You've got this girl head over heels. ☆"

"Hweh?! Wh-wh-what do you…?"

"He was pretty cool."

"You too, Tsukasa?!"

Akatsuki's eyes went wide over his ally's sudden betrayal.

However, Tsukasa wasn't joking…

"He gallantly arrived in our moment of need with the moon at his back, then distracted and neutralized an entire enemy watch-tower. Between that and the smoke bombs he used to plunge the hostile infantry into disarray, he provided us with a huge amount of support. What's more, he did so while fighting through his fear and not letting it show. It's no wonder they call him Japan's pride of the entertainment world."

"Wh-wh-wh—?"

"Without you, our plan to storm the castle would have undoubt-edly failed. You really are an incredible man," Tsukasa concluded.

"Oh, absolutely. You were so dashing back there, Akatsuki!" Lyrule agreed.

"Th…thanks…Akatsuki…," Ringo stammered.

"I, uh… ~~~~~~~~"

…and he wasn't alone. Lyrule and Ringo had also accompanied the rebel army, and when they piled on the praise and gratitude, Akatsuki's cheeks—which were normally as white and smooth as the driven snow—turned bright red.

He was accustomed to adulation for his illusions, but praise for who he was as a person was different. For a moment, he was struck speechless by the unfamiliar embarrassment.

"O-oh, hey, uh, Keine! Now that I think about it, there are still a bunch of injured people in Yamato. Are you sure it's all right for you to come with us?"

Akatsuki desperately shifted the topic and his gaze over to Keine in an attempt to escape.

Shinobu grinned. "What, feeling a little self-conscious?"

"Yeah! Yeah, I am! That's why I'm trying to change the subject!"

Keine gave the magician an understanding smile. "That's a fair question. You're certainly right that there are still many wounded, but now that I've gone through and stabilized all those in need of urgent care, I can entrust the rest to the Yamato physicians."

"But back in the Gustav domain, it took way longer to treat everyone."

"There, the underlying issue was the patients' poor physical conditions. By and large, their bodies lacked the strength to heal. They required constant bedside attendance. In contrast, the people of Yamato are generally hale and fully nourished. With their wounds properly sterilized and bandaged, the majority of the wounded will recover on their own. Nobody is going to die on account of my absence."

"Oh, I see," Akatsuki replied. "Well, that's good to hear… I'm sick of people having to die."

©Sacraneco

"You treated them quickly. You have our thanks." The quiet yet firm words of gratitude came from the young *byuma* woman sitting in the rearmost seat—the bodyguard and escort, Yamato's Samurai General Shura. "To win back our independence, we'll need the strength to stand up to the empire again. Your aid in getting our soldiers fighting fit has been a huge help."

"As a doctor, I would prefer that no combat took place at all, but...I recognize that the only way that can happen is if Yamato presents a military large enough to make the empire think twice about carrying out their invasion. It's a sad situation, but it is reality."

"I also put Bearabbit in charge of repairing and reinforcing your frontline defenses," Tsukasa added. "By the time Grandmaster Neuro finds out that he's lost Yamato, gets his lords together, and deploys his army, Bearabbit will have things well fortified."

If Yamato put on a big-enough display of force, it might dissuade Freyjagard from reclaiming the nation. After all, it had barely managed to control Yamato the first time around. Neuro was one thing, but the Freyjagard lords probably weren't too excited about another invasion.

Tsukasa went on, saying, "If you manage to get Freyjagard to the negotiating table, we're prepared to use our position as the Seven Luminaries who preach equality for all to censure the empire for condoning Mayoi's unjust governance and to assist Yamato in securing its independence diplomatically."

"Ever since our war of reclamation, we seem to find ourselves in your debt repeatedly. As Yamato's samurai general, I offer you our gratitude. Thank you, truly."

Shura bowed gratefully ...

...but when she raised her head, her expression was gloomy.

"And I'm sorry. After all you've done for us…we've yet to return the favor. I wish we could have provided Aoi with a better blade…" Shura turned to the seat beside hers and glanced at the weapon Aoi carried.

The sword's name was Mikazuki, and its sheath was lapis lazuli blue with delicate gold filigree. Aoi had required a new blade to replace Hoozukimaru, and Kaguya had gifted Mikazuki to her as thanks for her part in the war. Mikazuki was a fine weapon, but there was a good reason why Shura gazed at it so apologetically. Unlike Byakuran and Hoozukimaru, Mikazuki lacked the strength to withstand the full range of Aoi's techniques.

"There is little sense pining over that which does not exist," Aoi replied. "Besides, while Mikazuki may be inferior to Byakuran and Hoozukimaru, it is still a magnificent blade in its own right. Even if it cannot endure my full power, wielding eighty percent of my strength will still allow me to fight comfortably, that it will."

To Aoi, there was no need for Shura to look so sorry. She understood that the Yamato government had given her the greatest endowment it could. At the moment, Mikazuki was the mightiest sword in all of Yamato. It was a blade that, by all rights, should have belonged to the samurai general, yet it was given to Aoi instead. Aoi felt bad seeing Shura look so dejected over the gift.

As a matter of fact…

"I, too, am sorry for relinquishing something akin to one of your national treasures to Shishi."

…Aoi felt she ought to be the one apologizing. During the fighting, she gave the sword Shura lent her to their foe Shishi.

Shura shook her head. "Byakuran wanted to return to him. I know that better than anyone. There's no need for remorse. Actually…I'm grateful."

There was a hint of pity in her expression, but it was accompanied by a definite tenderness. Shura had once snapped, *"No talking about him,"* and refused to mention Shishi, but she was a different person now.

Learning the truth about Yamato during Kaguya and Tsukasa's tea party had shaken her so badly that she'd fled from the room. However, she ultimately came to terms with what being Yamato's samurai general meant, just as Kaguya expected. In the process, her feelings about her father changed, too.

"I have nothing to offer in return, but I intend to make up for it by working hard to keep you all safe."

"Thank you, Shura," Tsukasa replied. "I feel better knowing you have our backs."

Then it was time.

"We're…here," Ringo said from the driver's seat, and the truck stopped.

When the group disembarked, they found a spread of dense, verdant trees in front of them that stretched as far as the eye could see. Adel's journal had spoken of a forest that concealed the elf village, and this was it.

Lyrule took a deep breath as she stepped off the truck. "It smells so *naturey*," she said in surprise.

The air there had a different quality than Elm's woods. It was more vibrant and intense. It was probably because of how many of the trees there were broad-leaved. Between them and the dense undergrowth, the forest was like a green void. They couldn't even see thirty feet in.

The primeval vista, untouched by the hands of civilization, was enough to give Akatsuki some pause. "W-wait, we're supposed to go in there on foot?"

Tsukasa nodded. "We certainly aren't getting the truck any farther."

"It's pretty darn overgrown in there," Shinobu noted. "You sure you know where we're going, Tsukes?"

"Adel's journal gives a rough idea of the village's whereabouts. Using that knowledge, we scanned Ringo's satellite photos until we tracked down the exact spot." The settlement was originally a secret, sequestered from the outside world, making it difficult to locate, even by orbital camera, but Tsukasa and the others had eventually succeeded. "I already logged the village into our GPS, so we don't have to worry about getting lost. If we head in now, we should arrive by tomorrow evening."

If Tsukasa could declare that with such confidence, then there was little room for doubt. Akatsuki believed in Tsukasa, but his expression remained skeptical. "I mean, even if we don't get lost... we'll still end up covered in bugbites, right? I don't like the sound of that one bit."

"The problem is that you're wearing shorts, Akatsuki, m'lord. Shall we lather you with mud before we go in?" Aoi offered.

"Mud?! I don't want to get all dirtied up; that sounds filthy!"

"Covering yourself in mud will protect against bugbites and sunburn, though," Lyrule explained.

"Wait, really?"

Aoi nodded. "Indeed. Back when I fought in the jungles of Southeast Asia, we all did battle drenched head to toe in mud. Carrying around bug spray would have increased our loads, and the higher air temperatures may well have made the cans explode. But mud doubles as camouflage, you see. It protects you from foes and beasts alike, that it does."

"I mean, I guess... But it's still mud..."

"I have insect repellent made from peppermint oil. Do you want some?"

"Whoa, Shura, you're a lifesaver! Thanks!" Akatsuki replied.

"Yo, hook up your girl Shinobu, too. Mud would mess with my makeup something *nasty*. Ringo, you want in on this party?"

"Y...yes, please!"

Peppermint essential oil drove off bugs, and with how often Yamato soldiers had to do battle in their nation's mountain forests, they never left home without the stuff. Everyone shared Shura's supply and dabbed it on their exposed skin.

Once they were about finished...

"Are we ready, then?"

...Tsukasa addressed the group.

After everyone gave the okay...

"All right. Then I'll take point."

...he took the lead and guided the group through the thickets and into the deep, dark forest.

Ahead stood the elf village, and hopefully the Prodigies would uncover the world's secrets there.

At the same time, there was a small hubbub over in the Republic of Elm.

The thing was, some Seven Luminaries angels—Shinobu and Co.—had stormed an Elm detention facility to bust out Shura and Kaguya. The angels were supposed to be on Elm's side, yet they'd committed an egregious crime.

Now the national assembly had to decide what to do about it.

However, it really was just a *small* hubbub, and that was because, in their heart of hearts, the people of Elm always knew the angels would eventually leave them. This day was bound to come, and by actually attacking Elm, the angels gave Elm the option to cut ties with them. They didn't want to get in the way of Elm's independence.

Assembly Speaker Juno thought it was very like them to make such a move, but at the same time, she felt their concern was unnecessary. Since the election, Elm was determined to walk on its own two feet. The angels shouldn't have worried. The Freyjagard Empire's governance of Yamato was inhumane, and Elm hadn't condemned it out of a desire to suck up to Tsukasa and the other Prodigies. The assembly had mulled over and discussed it, and in the end, they made a choice they believed was their nation's will. At this point, having the angels offer an easy out for Elm to distance itself from them didn't change much. Elm's national assembly was going to act with unified resolve and do whatever felt necessary.

News was that the empire's civil war had ended, and Neuro ul Levias had emerged victorious on behalf of the existing regime. It wouldn't be long before Freyjagard reacted to Elm's decision. The fledgling democracy had made it clear that it would stand by the ideology of equality for all, and now it was time to see what the largest autocracy in the world had to say about that.

Depending on how it all shook out, there was a good chance that Elm's relationship with Freyjagard would sour.

If so, Elm had to ensure the safety of the imperial exchange students. There were basic humanitarian reasons to do so, of course, but allowing students specifically invited into the country to get hurt would stain Elm's reputation. Thus, the national assembly elected to take preventive measures and moved the exchange students to a heavily defended state guesthouse.

For all the supposed outward benevolence, this was a strictly political move. The students in question found the measures stifling. Considering the restrictions on when they were allowed to go outside, it was hard to blame them for feeling like they were under house arrest.

Presently, Elch was visiting the state guesthouse's lounge in his capacity as a state bureaucrat and apologizing to Nio Harvey and Cranberry Diva, two of the imperial exchange students, about the current state of affairs.

"I'm really sorry about all the hassle. We doubt that anyone would actually come after you guys just because you're from the empire, but we can't afford to take any chances."

Nio was well versed in matters of state, and he responded to Elch's apology with understanding. "Oh, don't think anything of it. We appreciate the Elm government's concern."

However, there was a hint of gloom in his polite smile. Cranberry was sitting beside him, and her expression was sullen as well.

Such reactions were entirely reasonable.

Studying abroad kept Nio and Cranberry out of direct danger, but their homeland was still going through unprecedented turmoil.

"From what we've heard, the Bluebloods were wiped out. Are…are your families okay?" Elch inquired after drinking some black tea.

The two students nodded.

"My family should be fine," Cranberry said. "Those Blueblood fuddy-duddies were all stuck in the past—no eye for progress. We Divas never got along with them in the first place."

"And I come from a line of knights all loyal to Emperor Lindworm, so we've never had any ties to the Bluebloods, either," Nio added.

"Oh, that's good to hear," Elch replied.

Had their families sided with the Bluebloods and fallen out of the current regime's favor, Elm would have to shelter the students until they could return home safely. Fortunately, that wasn't the case. And it was comforting to know that the two students hadn't lost their families while away from home.

Elch breathed a sigh of relief. "Well, even if Elm and the empire come to blows, we'll still make sure you get back home to your families safely, so you don't need to worry about anything on that front."

The comment earned a grim smile out of Nio. "That's good to hear, though I do hope it doesn't come to that. I still have a lot I'd like to learn from Elm."

"Yeah, me too," Cranberry agreed. "Say, Nio, do you really think the empire would start a war while we're still here?" There was no joy in her expression.

Nio sank into thought. "Hmm... That's a good question. Honestly, it's hard to say *what* Freyjagard will do. Things are probably still muddled in the wake of the insurrection."

"B-but we nobles couldn't even control Yamato in the first place. Won't everyone see this as a golden opportunity to give it up and be free of the responsibility?"

"There are definitely going to be people who view the situation that way, yes. The problem is, will the imperial nobles' pride allow them to take that option?"

"Yeah, you've got a point," Elch agreed. "The empire just lost all its northern territories. If they lose Yamato and the massive chunk of land it represents to the east on top of that, the first thing the emperor does when he returns from his New World expedition could be to chop Grandmaster Neuro's head off. The land may not be that valuable, but they can't just relinquish it completely..."

"And also...," Nio added, "I don't have any idea why the Four Grandmasters act as they do."

"Huh?" Elch replied.

"What do you mean?" Cranberry asked.

"To put it bluntly, we knew there was no value in occupying Yamato since before the war. Emperor Lindworm only invaded on the insistence of the grandmasters."

In other words, Yamato could be incredibly valuable in a secret way.

If so, there was no way the empire would back down. If worse came to worst, the situation could devolve into an all-out war.

With the Bluebloods defeated, Neuro held all the authority, and he was one of the grandmasters who'd pushed for seizing Yamato initially.

When they realized that, the mood in the room sank like a rock.

Nah, c'mon.

Elch shook his head. He couldn't let things get depressing. "Hey, look, there's no sense in worrying ourselves sick over stuff we have no way of knowing. More importantly, is there anything you two need to make your stay easier? The Elm government's not trying to obstruct your education or anything. If there's stuff you need to keep learning, then by all means, let me know. I'll do what I can to get it for you."

"I appreciate the concern," Nio replied. "Personally speaking, I have free access to the library, and the government officials and other people are helping me with my surveys, so I'm all set."

"What do you mean, *'surveys'*?"

"I'm trying to trace back the contents, processes, and outcomes of all the provisional government's policies so I can aggregate them and come up with my own interpretation of Mr. Tsukasa's ideology when he devised them. The more I work, the more I'm reminded of how nations really are formed from the connections among their citizens."

"But Freyjagard's an autocracy, right? Doesn't that make it pretty different from Elm, what with how everything feeds back to the emperor and all?"

"Oh, not at all. All governance systems require many people to keep everything in working order. Look at the present situation: His Grace put Grandmaster Neuro in charge of running the country while he's off on his expedition."

Nio posited that there were tons of things to be learned.

"Mr. Tsukasa made a lot of decisions that looked rash but ultimately bore fruit—chief among them being his revolution against the Freyjagard Empire. The more I study his actions, the more I believe that he views the causal relationships between governments and people differently than most others. We tend to operate off vague impressions, hopes, predictions, and personal rules of thumb, but his actions seem rooted in something deeper. After all, Mr. Tsukasa isn't the kind of person to risk other people's lives without a firm, logical reason."

"I mean, he's probably just that sure of his and the other angels' skills. With a team like that, who wouldn't be?"

"I don't think that's right."

"Huh?"

"Mr. Tsukasa wasn't confident at all. It was only over a short period, but I worked closely enough with him to discern that much. He had no self-confidence whatsoever and stewed over his decisions more than anyone I've ever seen. He *agonized*... But at the end of it all, he was still willing to take the initiative on all sorts of bold moves, and he made sure that they succeeded. My hypothesis is that he wasn't relying on luck or experience. Rather, he processes political phenomena through models that are almost mathematical in nature."

"...?"

"If you take political happenings as the aggregate of a series of strategic interactions among individuals and organizations all acting in their own self-interest, then devise a method to model those interactions mathematically, you can simulate the future without any sort of special talent or magic. Such a capability would be a huge boon to His Grace's government."

"That sounds...cool?"

"Oh-ho-ho! Nio is putting in some fine work, but I won't be bested that easily," Cranberry declared. "After inspecting and assembling the blueprints for the angels' generators and machines so many times, I've got them packed into my brain backward and forward! Now it doesn't matter if I return to Freyjagard! I can re-create those designs whenever I want! Once I join the imperial workshops, I'll have Freyjagard modernized in a flash!"

"Dang, that is impressive."

"And that's not all! Once Freyjagard is ready, I'll set up a special laboratory specifically for Panjandrum research! We'll start with the winch Panjandrum I made to storm that fortress, then build Flying Panjandrums with wings on their wheels that'll let them float. Next will come reinforced armored Panjandrums with even more smashing power and, someday, even remote Panjandrums controlled via electronic waves! Fighting wars in person will become a thing of the past and viewed as an act of barbarity! You heard me! The Panjandrum will bring world peace! Do you get it?! You get it; I see it in your eyes!"

©Sacraneco

"I'm sorry. I really don't get it."

The only thing Elch understood was that the imperial workshops would have his condolences if Cranberry got them researching those crazy things.

Still, though...

Setting aside that last bit of nonsense, it was clear that these two had passion to spare, and they'd turn it into results.

Honestly, should I be worried?

Elch had initially planned on giving them a pep talk, but now he didn't even want to. The fact of the matter was, when these two helped usher in a new era for Freyjagard, Elch and his fellows would end up as direct competitors.

"It sounds like when you two get back to the empire, you're gonna make Freyjagard more formidable than ever. Guess I can't afford to slack off, either."

Upon feeling the total weight of their enthusiasm, Elch focused up as well.

Then an interruption arrived.

"Vice Minister, you need to hear this! W-we've got trouble!"

The lounge door flew open, and a *byuma* staff member charged in.

"What's going on? You look like you just saw a ghost."

It had to be something big for the staffer to barge in without knocking, so Elch prioritized the situation over scolding the man for rudeness.

The staffer replied with his face ashen...

"W-we just received word from the Freyjagard Empire. Grand-master Neuro ul Levias has issued a formal reply to our resolution of condemnation, and..."

...whispering in Elch's ear so as not to be heard by the two exchange students.

When Elch heard the news...

"Wh-WHAT?!?!"

...his face turned as pale as the staffer's.

A full day had passed since the Prodigies entered the forest in search of the elf village.

As they progressed through the woods, the scenery changed. Perhaps it was something in the soil, but the trees were getting taller. Many were easily thirty or forty feet high.

"Whoa," Shinobu cooed. "Check it out, Lyrule. Their leaves form a dome that covers up the whole sky. How cool is that?"

"Oh, you're right. Elm Village sits deep in the mountains, but I've never seen trees so gigantic. My guess is that their growth is tied to the huge number of spirits in the area."

"Is that right?"

Lyrule responded to Keine's question with a nod, then strained her long ears for the spirit voices that only she could hear. "This is the first time I've ever felt so many gathered in the same place. And they're...they're all so happy."

As Tsukasa listened to the conversation, he double-checked their location on his smartphone. The rows of trees towering before them bore a striking resemblance to the sketches Adel had made of the area around the village, and according to Tsukasa's GPS, they were practically in spitting distance of their destination. He looked up and carefully scanned around to make sure he didn't miss anything as they walked.

After carrying on like that for a little while...

"Bingo."

...he spotted something unnatural. Sitting between the massive timbers was a series of wooden posts and a stone wall. The entire thing was overgrown with ivy.

They were fences designed to keep out wild animals. And if there were fences, then at some point, someone must have been there to build them.

When the party got closer, they saw the ruins of what had been buildings dotting the area beyond. Now there was no doubt.

"This is the elf village described in the journal."

After spending an entire day traveling deep into the forest, the group had finally reached its destination.

However...

"So this... This is where my mother and father used to live..."

"At long last, we're here. But..."

...not a single one of them cheered to celebrate their accomplishment.

"I wasn't expecting this place to look so demolished... It's like there was a big fire or something."

Akatsuki had a point. The majority of the settlement had been incinerated, rather than slowly weathered and weakened by rot. It almost felt like a modern-art exhibition.

Keine tilted her head in confusion. "Did they set fire to the village when they abandoned it, I wonder?"

"Nah, that's not it," Shinobu replied. She pointed at the charred ruins with a grim look on her face. "Look, the ivy hasn't climbed very high up the burned sections yet, even though the fences surrounding the village are absolutely covered in the stuff."

"A keen observation," Aoi remarked.

"And if you look closer...see here?"

Shinobu dug two of her nails into the remains of what was previously the facade of a house, then scraped them across its surface.

When she did, something fine and threadlike came free, then crumbled to pieces.

"Burned ivy?"

Shinobu nodded at Akatsuki. "That's right. This place was covered in vines when it was burned. All the green stuff on the ruined sections is relatively fresh. The fire happened within the last two or three years."

In other words...

"You're saying that the elves didn't set the village aflame when they left for the New World more than a decade ago, and that it occurred more recently?" Tsukasa asked.

"Exactly," Shinobu replied. "And it was done on purpose. Otherwise, it would have spread beyond the village."

Tsukasa agreed with the assessment. He gazed up at the canopy of leaves covering the sky. Little rain ever made it down there, so if the fire had started naturally, it would have spread to the woods around the settlement. The entire region would have been swallowed in the blaze. Examining the ruins suggested the fire was contained to the houses.

In short, somebody had come to this abandoned village and manually controlled the scope of the burn. And there was only one group of people who would have done that.

"This was the work of the evil dragon's followers, then."

Lyrule had inherited the evil dragon's seal, and the elf-village heads had referred to enemies seeking to hunt her down and release their master. The only question was, who exactly were these foes?

Tsukasa already had a pretty good idea of the culprits.

There was *one group* that fit the bill.

One group aggressively invaded Yamato when there was little economic gain from doing so.

One group was currently in the New World *as though in pursuit of the elves.*

"…"

However, all of that was conjecture based on circumstantial evidence. Tsukasa didn't have any hard facts.

Getting proof was part of why he and the others were here.

"Looking at all this, I dunno if the sacred tree is still standing," Shinobu remarked.

"According to the journal, the tree the elves treated as Yggdra lies deep within the village. We should investigate for ourselves," Tsukasa said.

Everyone moved more quickly than they had before.

They walked through the burned-out village, pressing farther into the ruined place. Eventually, the group passed the last of the buildings save for the fences, leaving them with nothing to guide their way except for stones underfoot.

The group carried on like that for about ten minutes. Then they arrived.

"What am I looking at?!"

"Whoa…"

A wide clearing about three hundred feet in diameter began at the end of the stone path, and at its center stood a mind-bogglingly enormous tree. It was surely twice as tall as the rest of the timbers, and its trunk had to be thirty feet thick, if not more. Naturally, a huge number of branches stretched from the trunk, and the leaves made up the three-hundred-foot forest clearing's entire canopy. There was so much green above that no sunlight could pierce through. Yet the glade was shockingly bright somehow. The earth and plants seemed to radiate a faint glow.

Tsukasa and the others realized that this place operated under rules beyond anything they understood.

"Is that...Yggdra's tree?"

A few gasped in astonishment.

However, *none craned their neck to look up at the tree's peak.*

No, it was the fantastical figure at the massive thing's base that commanded their attention.

Down at the base of the trunk were roots coiled around a giant limestone-white creature. The tree itself sat atop the quadrupedal entity's back. The creature, lying on the ground as though in repose, was unmistakable.

"Tsukes, that's, uh... That's a dragon, right?" Shinobu murmured.

Sure enough, the trapped animal bore a striking resemblance to the dragons of Earth legend.

"It seems...mummified," Shura remarked.

"It appears to be a good deal larger than the domesticated sort, that it does," Aoi noted.

"Look closer—you can see that it's been stabbed and shot with arrows," Tsukasa said.

"Is that...what killed it?" Ringo asked.

"I don't think so," Keine replied. "Just eyeballing it, I highly doubt the dragon sustained those injuries while alive. Someone attacked it after it was mummified."

Akatsuki gulped. "J-just tell me it's not gonna pull a jump scare and start moving around!"

The journal had referred to this glade as a sanctuary, but only the village leaders were permitted to enter. Adel knew only that the place was a big clearing with a holy tree. Gazing at the sight in person was awe striking. Everyone looked around with trepidation, save for one exception.

Huh…

Lyrule didn't feel any fear when she stared at the strange creature. As a matter of fact, it filled her with a sense of relief, as though she'd spotted torchlight amid a freezing blizzard.

"Lyrule?"

"…"

She found herself being drawn toward that feeling.

No, that wasn't quite it.

She was being *called.*

The voice was quieter than the spirits', but Lyrule could tell it was addressing her.

She followed the weak words and approached the dragon corpse.

"Lyrule, wait!" Tsukasa cried in alarm.

"It's okay," she replied; then she reached out.

Her fingers traced the tree roots, stopping upon the dragon's nose.

Boom. Jade-green light flew from the creature's body, accompanied by a surge of air.

"Ahhhhh!"

"Wh-wh-what's going on?!"

"Lyrule?!"

The torrent of light engulfed Lyrule, and although Tsukasa and the others tried to rush to her, they couldn't see a thing. The sheer volume of radiance blasted all color and contours from the world. Yet for how completely blinding it was, it wasn't painful to look at.

What in the world was going on?

As Shura and the Prodigies stood baffled, the glow subsided, and the world returned.

And there, right in the middle of it all, was Lyrule.

The wind had blasted her clothes to smithereens, and she

hovered in the air stark naked save for the gentle light wreathing her.

"You did well, Lyrule. Thank you for guiding them all the way here."

Lyrule's lips moved, and words came forth.
However...
"That's not Lyrule..."
As Keine pointed out, she wasn't speaking in Lyrule's youthful voice but with the timbre of an older adult woman.
Tsukasa recognized this tone.
"We meet again, Tsukasa."
Lyrule had been facing away from them, and she slowly turned around. And when her eyes came into view, Tsukasa saw that they glowed with *the same light they had once before.*
"So I was right, then. You were the one who contacted me back at Castle Findolph."
Lyrule—or rather, the entity borrowing her body—nodded.
Then...

"I imagine you've already figured it out by now, but allow me to properly introduce myself. My name is Yggdra. The Seven Luminaries adherents worshipped me as a god...and I'm the one who called you to this world to be the Seven Heroes."

...she revealed her identity.

Yggdra was known as the Seven Luminaries' deity, and legends placed her in stark opposition to the evil dragon.

Upon seeing her manifested through Lyrule…

"Whoa, I can't believe we're talking to an actual god."

"I figured this is where she'd be, if she existed at all, but still…"

…the Prodigies voiced their wonder.

Yggdra responded…

"You've come a long way and overcome so many trials to get here."

…by sweeping her gaze across the group and giving them a smile of utmost relief.

Oh, thank goodness.

Yggdra's battle with the evil dragon a thousand years ago had reduced the continent to ash, and she'd offered her life to form the literal foundation for its renewal. In her present reduced state, it had taken everything she had to call in a group of mighty people from one of the few nearby planets. Her *own* world was far more distant, and she could no longer call allies from home as she had a thousand years ago.

Yggdra had wondered whether this new group she summoned would be capable of standing against her foes.

The odds were undoubtedly grim.

And while the new Seven Heroes lacked the magic of Yggdra and her kin, they each possessed preeminent skills they'd used to brush aside every obstacle. Now they were here at last.

These champions might really be able to thwart her foes' ambitions.

There was still hope for this world.

Tears of relief began forming in Lyrule's—Yggdra's—eyes.

"I take it, then, that you've been watching us somehow," Tsukasa remarked.

"Indeed. I've been following you this whole time, observing through the dragon's eyes."

"You know, if you'd bothered to hold a proper conversation with us instead of spectating, we could have learned our reason for being here without traveling to the depths of this forest."

"*...I am sorry about that. I didn't realize how weak I'd grown. After summoning you all and imbuing you with a charm of shared languages, I found myself spent. I sincerely apologize for leaving you adrift in this world without a proper explanation.*"

Lyrule's lineage had strong ties to Yggdra, so the deity had tried to use her as an intermediary to communicate with the Prodigies, but she'd been too distant to give anything more than a brief message obscured by static.

But despite so little to go on...

"*Armed with nothing except a few legends and incomplete messages, you managed to find your way to me all the same. Now that you're here, I can converse with you just fine, even in my reduced state. Finally, I can tell you everything. I can explain why I have brought you...*"

Tsukasa closed his eyes for a moment in evident contemplation...

"All right, let's hear it. The whole truth with nothing held back."

...then snapped them back open.

His heterochromatic irises shone with clear resolve.

Yggdra nodded...

"*Of course. It's a fairly long story, but I'll make sure not to leave anything out.*"

"Oh, then never mind. If it's going to be long, we can just skip it."

"*Thank you for understanding. It all started about a thousand years ago, when we— Wait, what did you just say?*"

...but as soon as she began her tale, Tsukasa cut her off.

"*I'm sorry, WHAT?!*"

"You, um, you're saying...that you won't hear me out?!"

Yggdra seemed utterly flustered. That wasn't the answer she'd been expecting at all.

Tsukasa responded...

"Yeah, I think we can skip it."

...by repeating himself.

He was being serious. But the thing was...

"I—I, um, I would rather you didn't, though..."

...they weren't going to get anywhere like this.

Yggdra was at a complete loss.

"I'm not saying we can't talk. There are plenty of questions we're keen on asking you. But there's something you need to do first."

With that, Tsukasa took off his jacket and offered it to Yggdra.

"Put on some clothes. That body isn't yours."

It was a valid statement. When Yggdra had first possessed Lyrule, the force of the act had immodestly blown away Lyrule's outfit. It was unclear whether or not Lyrule was conscious of what was happening, but regardless, this was an embarrassing situation for a young woman.

Basically, Tsukasa was calling Yggdra out for her inconsideration of Lyrule.

"O-oh dear, I'm so sorry. I accidentally misadjusted my power a bit..."

Yggdra, having been thoroughly rebuked, hurriedly put an arm through one sleeve.

However, she was unused to operating human bodies, and the sleeve got caught. She wasn't having much luck getting the jacket on.

Tsukasa watched her struggle with a cold gaze. "...We've gotten

©Sacraneco

our hands on a fair bit of information throughout our journey here, and based on that knowledge, we've developed general conjectures about how this world operates, the events that led to the current situation, and what the evil dragon is."

"Oh. Y-you have?"

"Yes. Instead of having you explain from the ground up, I'd prefer to check our answers. After all, if my theories are true, then there's little time remaining."

Rather than waiting for Yggdra's response, Tsukasa dived into his exposition and laid it all out, as though in a hurry.

"After being unceremoniously dumped into this world, we had a few points of reference to work off to grasp our predicament. We theorized three rules governing this world based on Winona's story, our incomplete conversation with you, and the scattered knowledge of the Seven Luminaries we found across the continent.

"Rule 1: There existed some sort of threat to the world referred to as the evil dragon.

"Rule 2: There existed some sort of entity that opposed the evil dragon.

"Rule 3: There existed a group known as the Seven Heroes affiliated with the opposer that was called in from somewhere beyond.

"Everything you told us just now settled any doubts we might have had about rules two and three.

"Rule two refers to you, Yggdra, and three refers to the seven of us.

"Once you fill in those two, the first rule becomes obvious enough. After all, there just so happens to be a major power pursuing the elves, as it says in Adel's journal. The evil dragon and its followers...

＊　　＊　　＊

"...are none other than Blue Grandmaster Neuro ul Levias and the rest of the Lindworm dynasty."

"...!"

Yggdra's eyes went wide at Tsukasa's conclusion, and she gasped. Shock was written all across her face.

Tsukasa's hypothesis had hit the nail directly on the head.

Seeing Yggdra's expression was enough to assure Tsukasa he was correct, and he continued. "We've gathered information from the Seven Luminaries legends, the continent's recorded history, and Adel's journal. Based on that knowledge, I posit that the grand global affair went roughly like this: Approximately a thousand years ago, the world battled a threat that later came to be known as the evil dragon.

"If we consider that Neuro was telling the truth when he said he came from another world, we can assume that the evil dragon and its followers invaded from a planet separate from this one and Earth. One with highly developed magic.

"At that point, you and the elves joined forces and succeeded in putting down the incursion and sealing away the attackers. With that, the battle became nothing more than a legend from the distant past. However, Neuro and his cohorts were reincarnated as people from this world and now work to destroy the seal.

"That was why they made those overt acts of aggression against the economically insignificant nation of Yamato. They dispatched troops against the Freyjagard lords' wishes, yet when they won the region, they turned around and lazily subcontracted it as a self-governing dominion. The whole war seems illogical, but if Neuro and his contemporaries are the entities from rule one, it makes sense. They invaded Yamato in search of the elves who guarded the seal, but thanks to your warning, they had already left the continent for the New World.

"When Neuro and his allies arrived at the empty village, they discovered what happened and shifted Freyjagard's goal to pursue the elves. The New World expedition isn't to gather slaves or secure new territory; it's to catch the elves.

"Now, the elves saw the whole chase coming, so they entrusted the child bearing the seal, Lyrule, to Adel, and the empire's expedition fell for their diversion hook, line, and sinker. But I digress. The issue is that the elves' ploy won't work forever. The Lindworm administration invaded Yamato and the New World with extreme prejudice, and sooner or later, they *will* find their quarry. And while we have no way of knowing the elves' current situation, it's only a matter of time before their deception is exposed.

"And knowing that...you took action. You used Lyrule, just as you did at the feudal lord's castle and as you are now. Through her, you called people strong enough to oppose Neuro and his forces. And you ended up with seven earthlings."

Tsukasa paused briefly for effect...

"Now, that's my rough understanding of the events. Was there anything I got wrong?"

...then locked eyes with Yggdra.

Yggdra replied...

"*N-no, not at all. You nailed it! That's exactly what happened! All of it!*"

...by shaking her head.

Her voice rang with excitement. She was amazed.

Not only had Tsukasa identified the evil dragon and its followers, but he'd also deduced the major happenings with such accuracy that Yggdra couldn't find anything meaningful to correct. Her allies were proving themselves to be dependable indeed.

When Yggdra's eyes lit up with joy, Tsukasa's expression darkened. "So I was right, then? That's unfortunate. I hoped I wasn't."

The events he'd described would seriously impact things in the future. Tsukasa had worried this was the case and wished to be wrong.

However, now that he knew he was correct, he understood there was no time to waste lamenting his misfortune. "Then there's one more thing we need to ask you."

He stared pointedly at Yggdra and asked the most important question of all.

"Can you get us to our endgame?"

"I'm sorry, your...endgame?"

Tsukasa nodded. "I assume it goes without saying, but our first and foremost objective in this world is to find a way for the seven of us to return to Earth. Neuro has already offered that to us. Cooperating with him is one way to reach our endgame. If you want us to give that up, I assert you are obligated to offer another route to our goal. You called us here to be pawns in your campaign against Neuro. If we do that for you, will you return us to our original world?"

When Tsukasa finished his question, the whole lead-up to it finally clicked for Yggdra. It was a perfectly reasonable ask.

Naturally, the fact that Yggdra had called them there meant she could send them back, so she gave him a big nod...

"Yes, of course! I promise!"

"I don't believe you."

...and Tsukasa immediately rejected her assertion.

"What?!"

He completely shut her down.

Yggdra found herself at a loss. She returned Tsukasa's stare with a questioning look, noticing the frigidity in Tsukasa's hetero-chromatic eyes. The emotion there bordered on outright hostility.

Tsukasa believed he had a perfectly acceptable reason for feeling that way, though.

"Why should I trust you? After all, you *nearly killed us once*."

"*Oh...*"

"If not for the people of Elm, each of us would've perished in an alien world. There's no reason to trust the entity who put us in that position."

"*I—I, um...*"

Yggdra didn't know what to say to that. It was true that the Prodigies had been injured because of her flawed summoning, and that was something she could never take back. She had fought hard to keep them alive during the crash, but knowing they wouldn't have crashed if she hadn't summoned them weakened that excuse.

"What's more, you just told us you've grown weak. That was the whole reason you couldn't properly get in contact with us, right? I don't pretend to understand magic particularly well, but I have to assume that bridging the gap between worlds is more difficult than simply talking to someone far away. So I have to ask: In your current state, are you capable of returning us safely to our original world? I'd rather not get sent back just to find myself drowning in the middle of the Pacific."

Yggdra had already jeopardized the Prodigies' lives once, so Tsukasa had little faith in her abilities. He was the Prodigies' representative; his duty was to keep them all safe. Unless Yggdra offered some assurance, he couldn't justify relying on her.

And so...

"Do you have anything to allay my concerns? People *have* called you a god."

...he posed his inquiry again, more firmly than before.

Tsukasa wanted hard evidence that he could trust her.

But when he made his demand...

"..."

...Yggdra had no reply.

She'd been sincere when she promised to send the Prodigies home. There *was* a way to guarantee their safe return to Earth, but the method was single use. She couldn't afford to pull out her trump card now.

Unfortunately, her remaining power was insufficient to convince the Prodigies. She had given herself up to restore the continent, and as a result, she lacked the strength to even converse with others unless they came to the tree.

Yggdra couldn't solve this with a show of ability.

So what else could she do to win her champions' confidence? Yggdra thought it over...but failed. Nothing came to mind, not one solitary reason they should believe in her.

However, that was to be expected...

"You're right to be suspicious of me. I've done plenty to you all, of course, but fundamentally...I'm not the sort of being people trust. I lack the right."

"...?"

...and it gave Yggdra an idea.

One element about the Seven Luminaries went unrecorded, Yggdra's identity. If she told these people, they'd lose all confidence in her. Exposing that final truth would only end poorly for her. The Seven Heroes might refuse to cooperate at all.

Despite that, or perhaps even *because* of it...

If I have nothing to offer, then at the very least, I ought not to hold anything back.

If someone so untrustworthy desired help, the only thing to give was total honesty.

So, having made up her mind…

"Here's the truth. The elves called me a god, but I'm not anything so admirable.

"The evil dragon was a powerful mage called Father. He is from another world with highly developed magic and created a series of homunculi. Neuro is one of them…and so am I."

…she told the Prodigies of herself.

""""……!"""""

Yggdra's admission came as a surprise to everyone. Shock and wariness colored their features.

The air was so tense you could cut it with a knife.

However, Yggdra was prepared for that, so she continued her confession undeterred. *"More than a thousand years ago, our creator, Father, was shunned for his preeminent magical ability and keen mind. He was branded a heretic and exiled from his original world."*

As Neuro explained, science nearly ruined his and Yggdra's home world. From there, magic rose in prominence and achieved widespread use and adoption across their society.

The planet's history left its populace terrified of anything that might lead to major upheaval. And that fear manifested as persecution toward anyone with the skills capable of bringing about innovation. In Father's case, he was shunned from the world.

"That sent Father into a mad rage, and he came to this planet with me, Neuro...and three other homunculi. He swore revenge against the world that had rejected him, and it was here that he planned to create the military assets to carry out his vengeance."

Father required the ability to create soldiers of incredible strength—magic that would evolve his homunculi into beings on par with deities.

To make that a reality, Yggdra and the others took their existing research on forced evolution magic and used this new planet to master the craft. The endemic inhabitants became their test subjects.

They carried out inhumane experiments, the likes of which were unheard of on their homeworld. Yggdra spared the Prodigies no detail about the many casualties that came from those efforts. The scars of their world were still visible across the globe in the form of people with animal traits—*byuma*.

And that wasn't all.

Yggdra looked over at Shura, who'd been hanging back at the rear of the group. *"...You hail from Yamato, correct?"*

"...Who, me?" Shura asked.

"I owe you an apology. The tragedy that befell Yamato three years ago wouldn't have transpired if not for our research."

"What...do you mean?"

"Originally, we used the land of Yamato as a custodial facility for our flawed prototypes...the invalids whose minds broke when we forced their bodies to evolve. We held them in Yamato for later use as foot soldiers in our war of revenge.

"Their broken minds left them prone to random acts of violence, so to manage them efficiently, we injected them with special magic factors. Those would be what you call 'spirits.' Using a spell called

Administrative Authority allowed us to seize direct control of that group through those magic factors... I trust you understand what I'm getting at."

Shura gasped. "So you mean...Princess Mayoi's brainwashing was..."

"Precisely." Yggdra nodded. *"She was using Administrative Authority."*

Following the war one thousand years ago, Yggdra had given the elves access to Administrative Authority and the bell used to spread its power. In so doing, the elves could offer the experiment victims better treatment.

Yggdra described the fantastic efforts of the elves. They cared diligently for those so thoroughly wronged. After generations of intermixing with the naturally magically gifted and magic-resistant elves, the descendants of the test victims regained their sanity. Once they'd recovered enough, they founded their own nation on what was previously their cage.

"As more generations passed and elven heritage became scarcer, their magic waned, and knowledge of Administrative Authority and the bell was lost... Until a certain few who knew about those things were reborn in the modern era."

Yggdra was referring to Neuro and the other grandmasters— her old allies.

By taking advantage of those forgotten factors, they carried out a swift invasion of Yamato.

The dead of Yamato returned to the soil, spreading their magic factor until it became ingrained in the fabric of the nation as its "native spirits." Eventually, it took root in nearly the entire population, a consequence beyond what Yggdra had ever imagined. It spelled doom for Yamato.

"I'm truly, truly sorry."

"…"

Yggdra hung her head, yet she still spied Shura's tight fists. She clenched her fingers so powerfully that it restricted their blood flow.

Yggdra accepted that rage as justified. If she and her ilk had never existed, Yamato's tragedies would never have occurred. No amount of apologizing would right this.

"I am in no way deserving of being called a god. My kind have invited calamity in both the past and the present. After I began to doubt our mission, I informed our home world of Father's scheme and fought against him. And when this continent perished from the battle, I sacrificed my body to nourish it. That was my attempt at atonement… I confess a desire for forgiveness motivated me."

Apologizing to get the people you'd irreparably harmed to absolve you was an act of base narcissism. It succeeded in making only the wrongdoer feel better. And that was all Yggdra had done. At first.

"But not anymore."

Yggdra lifted her head.

No longer was her expression one of remorseful weakness. The eyes upon her carried everything from caution to scorn to outright hatred, but she faced them with dignity.

"I've spent a long time—a thousand years—existing alongside this world and watching its people go about their lives.

"They stood atop the ashes and ruins of this broken land, tilled the wasteland, erected houses, and built villages.

"I saw people helping others, groups coming together to aid individuals.

"My kin and I were built to be powerful, and these creatures' strengths paled compared to ours. But they came together and lived more resolutely than we ever could have dreamed.

"There were atrocities committed across their history, of course. Deeds so vulgar as to make you look away. Not everything I witnessed was beautiful. Yet even amid such adversity, the people carried themselves gallantly. As I bore witness, I felt a desire building.

"I wished to protect them.

"I wanted to safeguard the chain of lives that went unbroken for so long and everything else I observed here. Not for atonement this time, no, but for the sake of a warmer, larger emotion. One that I lack the words to describe!"

Yggdra was willing to do anything to achieve that end. Laboring for it made her feel capable of anything.

And so…

"Presently, I'm not strong enough to stop the imminent threat.

"I poured most of my power into this land's foundations. My remaining strength is but a sliver.

"You traveled to my side after I put you in danger and left you adrift in a foreign world, yet I have nothing to offer in exchange for your trust. In this borrowed body, I can't even lower my own head to demonstrate my sincerity.

"I have nothing. No might, no natural form, and no time. But still, my desire to protect this world's people is genuine! Please, you have to believe me! I implore you to lend me your strength and help me accomplish what I'm not strong enough to do on my own!"

To make her plea, Yggdra laid everything bare.

Instead of bowing with her borrowed body or trying to trick

Tsukasa and the others by lying about her powers, she voiced her raw feelings.

It didn't benefit her to do so, and she had no proof of her claims. Tsukasa had asked her to give him something he could trust, and she'd failed.

However...

"H-hey, Tsukasa!"

...words were a vessel that carried emotions. And those spoken from the heart had the power to touch others.

"Look, I, uh...I think we can trust this god lady."

The first one to speak up was Akatsuki—the most cowardly boy of them all.

"I mean, she did put us in a pretty rough spot, a really rough spot. And our lives would've been way easier if she hadn't, but... The way I see it, there are times when you don't have a choice but to ask for help, even if you know it's going to make the other person's life complicated."

And that was even truer when you were the only one capable of even asking for aid.

"Yggdra wanted to protect people but knew she was weak and understood she couldn't do anything alone. Still, she really wanted to help... That seems like a good reason to bring us here, don't you think?"

And when Akatsuki finished...

"Tsu...kasa...I think...that if...we have to choose...between the two endgames...then I'd like...to trust Yggdra..."

...Ringo followed after him.

"Oh?" Tsukasa replied.

"After all...Neuro might...not...have been lying, but..."

Ringo thought back to how Neuro had acted during the peace talk in Astarte.

The emperor had entrusted Neuro with governing the empire, yet he'd agreed to arguably terrible terms for Freyjagard. He'd surrendered with a pleased grin. His acceptance was a great boon to Elm, but the behavior rubbed Ringo the wrong way.

The genius inventor had spent ages watching someone work himself to the bone to protect the rights and interests of his people. Neuro was different from Tsukasa, however. He wasn't the sort to lift a finger for others. Tsukasa's keen insight determined that Neuro had been truthful when he claimed he could send the Prodigies home, and although Ringo believed him...

"I'd still be scared...to put my life in the hands...of someone who only cares about himself."

Next was Aoi. "I concur with Akatsuki and Ringo, that I do." She closed her eyes as though recalling something. "Those in great need are often those least able to offer recompense. Yet theirs are the pleas that chivalry calls on us to answer."

Beneath her eyelids, she saw the war-torn regions she'd marched across as a prodigy swordmaster.

People who had nothing were the ones who needed the most help. Aoi understood that better than most. They had nothing to give in return but thanks, and that was precisely why they needed saving.

From there...

"The bottom line is, if Lyrule is that important for Neuro's goal or whatever, then negotiating with him isn't a realistic option for us."

"He and his allies want to destroy the seal she carries. The journal described the process as 'tearing her soul to shreds,' which doesn't sound pleasant. Knowing that, it's hard to imagine us working together."

...Shinobu and Keine expressed their de facto support for Yggdra as well.

According to Yggdra's story, Neuro threatened Lyrule's safety, so allying with him was out of the question.

Shinobu shot Tsukasa a biting look. "However, you already knew all that, didn't you? You asked Yggdra those mean questions to give her a chance to win *us* over."

"..."

"C'mon, Tsukes, give us *some* credit. None of us wants to go home if it means sacrificing Lyrule or this world's people to do it."

That was an issue they'd settled back when Masato left.

"Besides," Shinobu continued, "if the whole get-Yggdra-to-send-us-home plan turns out to be a bust, we can always find another way to get back once we've saved Lyrule and the rest of the world. I'll find us that way home if I have to turn over the entire continent to do it. And if even *that* doesn't work out, ol' Ringo here can build us a boat that can sail across worlds!"

"Y-yeah. I'll see...what I can do!" Ringo agreed.

Aoi nodded. "And in the meantime, I shall keep you all safe, that I shall."

"And I intend to ensure that no matter what circumstances befall us, our health will remain in tip-top shape," Keine added.

"And I, uh...I can cheer you all on! Yeah!" Akatsuki said.

All of them felt the same as Shinobu.

There was a wicked plot brewing, and the Prodigies had no intention of leaving without thwarting it first, especially not with Lyrule's life on the line. That was never an option.

Five gazes fell on Tsukasa, each pair of eyes burning with resolve, kindness, and drive.

Tsukasa took them all in...

"Well, okay then."

...and smiled for the first time since arriving at the great tree.

He faced Yggdra once more…

"Yggdra, I believe in you as well. If you've earned the trust of both my steadfast allies and a millennium's worth of elves, then that's good enough for me."

…and offered his hand.

At the sight…

"Thank you…"

…Yggdra cried joyous tears.

After they exchanged a hard, firm handshake, Tsukasa turned to his friends. "This journey of ours has felt like a wild goose chase for the longest time, but now we have our final objective. We're going to crush the Freyjagard Empire and the Lindworm administration's ambitions, save Lyrule and the world, and, once we're finished, use Yggdra's power to return to Earth. This will be an all-or-nothing scenario—and I'll be counting on each one of you more than ever."

The others nodded in answer. Their eyes gleamed, and they understood what they needed to do.

That moment marked the quiet beginning of the High School Prodigies' final battle.

"Okay, so we've decided that our big goal is to stop Neuro and his buddies at any cost, but now that we've got our mission, I'd like to get more concrete details on the situation."

Now that they'd decided to work with Yggdra, Shinobu made a recommendation.

"We know now that Neuro and the other grandmasters are trying to revive your dad, the so-called evil dragon, but what are they

©Sacraneco

planning on doing to Lyrule to achieve that? Our tactics depend on their exact strategy."

"*That's a good point,*" Yggdra replied. "*Right now, Father's soul is locked away with the cycle of reincarnation that revolves around this world. The seal has been passed down and inherited by elves for generations, and now it resides within this body, etched onto Lyrule's soul. By killing her, they can break the seal, and Father will be reborn. I'm certain that's their goal. Now, as far as what form the reincarnation will take, it appears that the grandmasters intend to use Emperor Lindworm von Freyjagard as Father's vessel.*"

"Wait, the emperor's body?" Akatsuki asked.

"*That's right. Father's magic—his raw life energy—is so powerful that putting his soul into an average body would be like cramming an ocean in a wineglass. It wouldn't take long at all for it to break. That is why the grandmasters haven't been able to make their move for the past thousand years.*

"*Sometimes, though, the world produces a prodigy whose abilities outstrip their era, just as my old world produced Father. And Lindworm von Freyjagard is one such exception. His magic transcends even the elves'. Between that and his mighty body, he's the only person who could possibly serve as a vessel for Father.*"

"But...what'll happen to the emperor if they pull it off?"

Yggdra's expression darkened at Akatsuki's inquiry. "*Two souls can't coexist in a single body for any prolonged period. When Father is revived, the emperor's persona will quickly be overwritten and cease to exist.*"

"Really? They'd do that to their own emperor?"

"Have the grandmasters no loyalty as retainers?" Aoi asked.

"*They...believe themselves to be superior to the people of this world.*"

Yggdra surmised that her kin probably thought of this world's people as little more than lab rats.

Tsukasa posed a question. "I know that Emperor Lindworm's been using the Four Grandmasters—this 'Father' character's minions—since before he took the throne, and it was supposedly their counsel that led him to invade Yamato, but... Based on his behavior, it would appear that he doesn't know they intend to use him as a vessel."

"No. Or at least, probably not. If he did, I doubt he'd go along with their plan to invade Yamato or depart for the New World."

Tsukasa nodded. "In that case, telling Emperor Lindworm the truth is one option we could explore."

Keine voiced her agreement. "Broadly speaking, there are three options we can select from. We can make sure Lyrule stays safe, defeat Neuro and the other grandmasters, or render the vessel unusable. Any one should suffice."

"B-but...!" Then, unexpectedly, Ringo offered her doubts. "When the grandmasters...fought Yggdra...all those years ago... they destroyed...the whole continent...right? Will we really...be able...to beat them?"

According to the legend of the Seven Heroes, the villains reduced the entire continent to a wasteland. Ringo's fears were entirely reasonable. However...

"I wouldn't fret about that."

...Yggdra wasn't worried.

"Now that they've reincarnated, the grandmasters are nothing more than normal humans. *Their original forms evolved to supernatural levels like my corpse here, but those bodies have been lost."*

The grandmasters had knowledge yet lacked sufficiently powerful forms to take full advantage of it.

"The magic they know is beyond anything this world has discovered, so they're certainly a force to be reckoned with, but it's nothing your scientific and military capabilities won't be able to overcome."

"R-really?! Oh, that's such a huge rel—"

"But..."

"There's a but?!"

Before Akatsuki could get too comfortable, Yggdra cut him off, wearing a serious look. *"There's one thing you need to watch out for: the Philosopher's Stones."*

"The...Philosopher's Stones, you say?"

"Tsu...kasa...is she talking...about...?"

Keine and Ringo looked questioningly at Tsukasa, who nodded. "I suspect so."

Yggdra's descriptor was a bit melodramatic, but Ringo and Keine both had a pretty good idea of what objects she referred to.

"Are you alluding to the *black crystals* we found embedded in Elm's Lord of the Woods, Gustav, and the Yamato wolf Shiro?" Tsukasa asked.

Keine and Ringo had extracted a sample of the strange mineral from Gustav's chest, and when they used it on a rat, the crystal forced its body tissue to mutate. Whatever that stuff was, it didn't exist back on Earth.

Yggdra bobbed her head in the affirmative. *"I am. Philosopher's Stones are coagulated bits of blood and flesh that fell from Father during our war a thousand years ago. To exact revenge on our home world, we intended to use this planet as a place to evolve into more powerful organisms. We modified cells, transplanted genes from other capable entities... That is how I obtained the body you see back there."* She gestured at the mummified dragon behind her. *"Once our bodies transformed, they became incredibly powerful down to the cellular level. We learned to induce that evolution in other beings by injecting them with our blood or transplanting our tissue. The process is capable of giving them incredible magical and physical abilities.* It can even *restore dead soil to its former glory."*

"So you're saying that if Neuro took that flesh and strengthened himself with it like he did Gustav..."

"Exactly. That would be a dangerous situation indeed. However, using Father's cells to force evolution places a tremendous burden on the subject. Without an iron will or a hardy body like an elf's, the subject will succumb to the strain and crumble. And now that the grandmasters are mere humans, the cells would affect them as they would anyone else. I doubt they'd willingly take that risk."

Tsukasa was reminded of the results when they applied the stone to the rat. The animal entered a state of heightened excitement, then died from elevated blood pressure, practically rupturing from the inside. It was hard to imagine anyone willingly accepting something like that into their body unless they truly had no other choice.

"So however we decide to thwart the grandmasters, we have to ensure it doesn't involve backing them into a corner. That isn't going to be easy."

With that being the case, doing something about Emperor Lindworm was starting to seem like the most enticing play available.

However, there was another issue that needed to be dealt with first.

"No matter what steps we take against the grandmasters, our primary course of action will always be the same."

"You mean..."

"You're talking about Massy, right?" Shinobu asked.

Tsukasa nodded. "That's right. Merchant chose to join Neuro, and we need to tell him what the grandmasters are plotting. Once he learns that Neuro's scheme involves killing Lyrule, he'll never stand for it."

There was no reason to stay on Neuro's good side anymore. Tsukasa pulled out his smartphone. Before things got underway, he needed to figure out how to link up with Masato. Unfortunately...

"His phone's off."

"Did it run out of battery?" Akatsuki asked.

"He brought a charger with him, so I doubt it," Tsukasa said. "He might be sleeping or in the middle of something. Or...he might not be interested in keeping in contact."

"B-but why not?!"

"It's not surprising. The whole reason Merchant split from us was to maintain a strong relationship with Neuro. He won't chat us up while working into Neuro's good graces. Doing so would jeopardize what he's after, and I can't blame him for playing it safe. I'll send him a text and see how he—"

Just as Tsukasa was explaining things to Akatsuki and booting up his messaging app, he was interrupted.

"SCREEEEEE!!!!"

A shrill cry shook the sky above.

"Wh-what's with the cawing?!"

Everyone looked up in surprise, spotting a bird swooping toward them through a small gap in the overhead foliage.

"Is that...an eagle?"

When Shura spotted the animal—a white-shouldered eagle—she let out a shocked cry. "Foremost?!"

"A friend of yours?" Keine asked.

"We use eagles to pass messages while undercover. Foremost is the swiftest of all and only to be used in emergencies!"

Shura extended her arm, and the bird perched atop it, wrapping its thick talons firmly around her slender arm. There was a letter tied to one of its legs.

Shura unrolled it, scanned the contents...

"——!!!!"

...and gasped.

The message had come straight from Kaguya...

"The Freyjagard Army is massing troops on Yamato's border... one hundred and fifty thousand of them!"

...and described the empire's retaliation against Yamato.

Akatsuki's eyes bugged out at Shura's news. "A—a—a hundred and fifty *thousand*?! Isn't that, like, way more than they've sent at us before?!"

Shinobu gave Tsukasa a look. "Tsukes, a hundred and fifty thousand sounds a whole lot like—"

"I'm aware. I don't know how many died during the insurrection, but in all likelihood... With Freyjagard's big campaign going on, the odds are good that's every soldier the empire can muster."

Freyjagard had likely even rounded up soldiers who typically spent their time defending border checkpoints and guarding villages. Now that the empire had rooted out all internal dissidents, it could afford to pull audacious stunts like this.

"There are already around thirty thousand troops standing in battle formation at our old imperial border. They say that they're being dispatched to put down the rebel movement that threatens the self-governing dominion's rights and the empire's interests..."

Shura hesitated for a moment. "Apparently, Grandmaster Neuro ul Levias also claims...that you all are the 'ringleaders' and that if we turn you over, Freyjagard will consider the issue resolved and recognize Yamato's sovereignty."

Tsukasa sighed heavily. "Then my bad hunch was on the mark." *This* was why he'd told Yggdra they didn't have much time. "Neuro's figured out we made contact with Yggdra."

During the meeting with the Yamato dominion leadership, Jade had explained that Neuro ordered him not to rock the boat. Back then, Neuro had hoped he could get by without letting the Prodigies discover anything in Yamato he didn't want them to. That was why the dominion government had been so oddly cooperative initially.

However, Neuro wasn't going to get what he wanted.

Now that he suspected the Prodigies knew his objective—killing Lyrule—he pulled out all the stops and went on the attack.

"Reclaiming the dominion is merely a pretext that allowed him to mobilize that army. Neuro's true goal is to stick us with the blame for the dominion government's downfall so he can get rid of us," Tsukasa said.

"Don't worry," Shura replied. "Yamato won't sell you out."

"I appreciate that."

Shura was right; Kaguya wasn't going to hand them over.

Tsukasa didn't *hope* that she wouldn't. Rather, he *knew* she had to refuse.

It was obvious after some consideration. The bitter taste of imperial rule still lingered on every tongue in Yamato. None of Kaguya's subjects would believe any honeyed words from Freyjagard.

If anything, Kaguya would likely side with the Prodigies and fight the empire. Yamato was always going to cross blades with

Freyjagard if it genuinely wished to maintain independence. It was best to do so while they had a powerful ally in the Prodigies.

There was little chance of Yamato turning against Tsukasa and the others for the moment. And that being the case, they were in little danger. It was Masato, who was right by Neuro's side, whose well-being was in jeopardy. There was no telling when or how Neuro might use him as a hostage, so the other Prodigies needed to reunite with him quickly.

Unfortunately, Neuro was now entirely hostile, so any attempt to contact Masato could put him in danger. Phone calls were out of the question for the time being, and messaging could be perilous, depending on the situation.

That left only one option.

"Shinobu."

Tsukasa turned his attention to the master ninja journalist. That was all she needed to understand. She nodded. "Yup, I read you. You want me to sneak into the empire, then bring Massy and Roo out with me, yeah?"

"Can you do it?"

"I'm gonna be real with you. I can't offer you my usual guarantees. The bad guys know exactly how badly we want Massy out of there, and there's a good chance they'll have him under heavy guard."

"Then I shall accompany you," Aoi declared. "Conflict such as this is my specialty, that it is."

However, Shinobu shot her down. "Nah, that's not an option."

"Why not, may I ask?"

"They've marshaled a huge force, which means they're planning on more than making a threat. The grandmaster is acting under the assumption that we know what he's after. He's not gonna wait long. If Yamato doesn't immediately give us up, he'll come charging across the border. When that happens, we'll need you here in Yamato. There's no way for you to protect everyone, but if I go alone, then at least the five of you will be safe, even if things go south on my side. That's why you want me to do this solo, right, Tsukes?"

Shinobu looked over at Tsukasa, hoping he would back her up.

"You're correct about why Aoi needs to stay behind, but not about why I chose you for the job."

"Oh yeah?"

"I picked you because I'm confident that Shinobu Sarutobi, prodigy journalist, can overcome this challenge without help. In fact, I'm certain that you're the only person in the world capable of the feat."

Tsukasa wasn't trying to feed Shinobu's ego. He was speaking from the heart. No matter how impossible a task seemed, Tsukasa never doubted that she and the other Prodigies would succeed.

Never.

Tsukasa knew that he was an ordinary man who had no choice but to plan for every eventuality, and he couldn't place that sort of wholehearted faith in himself. But he could put it in them. Each of them possessed an incredible talent that exceeded the bounds of traditional sense.

Knowing that she had Tsukasa's complete trust...

"Heh-heh. I guess you do know me pretty well, then! There's not a place in the world that I can't infiltrate. You can sit back and leave it to your unstoppable girl!"

...Shinobu threw out her ample chest with pride.

It wasn't empty bravado.

"I had a feeling things might come to this... Okay, that's a bit of an exaggeration, but still, I laid some groundwork back when I was in the empire as a fake exchange student. Don't you worry. I'll get Massy and Roo out. So promise me this…"

Shinobu's eyes moved to each person assembled in the glade, her expression serious.

"When I bring 'em back, I want *all of you there* for the welcoming party."

She demanded they all survive.

There was really only one response.

"Of course."

With that, the Prodigies set their sights on their new endgame.

Most of them would remain in Yamato to confront the massive imperial army, while Shinobu snuck into the enemy stronghold alone to find Masato.

Each had their mission, and they were the best people for the jobs.

CHAPTER 2

⚔ The War Begins ⚔

"Whoo. It's really getting chilly."

The Imperial Gold Knight sighed as he gazed up at the twilit sky. His breath came out white, rising over the encampment on a hill along the old Yamato border.

"I swear, a couple of big shots decide they want to have a power struggle, and all of a sudden, it's all war all the time. I'm sick of this nonsense. I just wanna go home."

Winter was around the corner, and yet here they were, still fighting. He clicked his tongue. The whole year had been a mess from start to finish. If he'd known that this was how things would play out, he would've gone on that damn New World campaign. Stories claimed it was summer all year round over there.

As he grumbled, another Gold Knight standing beside him nodded in agreement...

"Look, we already beat the Bluebloods. We'll be home free if we can clean up this mess."

...and offered him some words of encouragement.

"That's a big if," the first man replied, laughing sardonically. "You think Yamato's gonna accept our demand?"

The question made his compatriot's expression darken. "Those honor junkies? Not a chance."

These two had fought in the previous Yamato war, and they knew all about the samurai way. Yamato's people weren't the sort to sell out their saviors.

Plus, if the rumors about the self-governing dominion maintaining itself via mind control were true, then the Yamato citizens were undoubtedly furious. It was painfully obvious they'd fight to the bitter end.

The battle ahead was shaping up to be a fierce one.

That said, it wasn't all bad news.

"But still, you heard about how big our army is, right? A hundred and fifty thousand soldiers, man. *A hundred and fifty thousand.* They even pulled in those watching the borders. We're talking all-out war. Yamato's got, what, ten thousand tops? Plus, that's not accounting for how exhausted they are after battling their own countrymen. This will be the easiest war ever."

"I mean, that's all true, but still, I dunno…"

As the two knights exchanged optimistic and pessimistic views, a soldier rushed up to them in a hurry. "Come quick! Yamato's White Wolf General is here as a messenger."

"Oh, huh. Can't say I expected the new samurai general to deliver the news in person."

The knights braced themselves. It was time.

There was only one reason she was here—to formally announce Yamato's reply to the demand Grandmaster Neuro sent yesterday.

"So what'd she say? Is Yamato refusing to submit like we suspected?"

"A-actually, about that!"

Yamato's answer was the last thing the knights had expected. Not a single one of the soldiers had seen this coming. A shocked stir ran through the crowd.

Six of the High School Prodigies stood pathetically, each stripped of their clothes and bound in iron chains.

"Are those supposed to be the angels?"

"What the hell? They're just kids. Is Yamato trying to pull a fast one on us?"

"No, no. Back when I was in Drachen, I saw them from a distance. I didn't get a great look, but that's definitely them there."

White Wolf General Shura was standing at the front of the procession, leading the Prodigies by the chain. She addressed the two knights. "I've brought you every angel in Yamato, just like you asked."

Princess Kaguya's new Yamato had betrayed its saviors and handed them over to the empire.

"Heh-heh. That's a smart choice you made. I didn't know you guys had it in you," said one of the Gold Knights.

"I guess having your country destroyed does teach you a lesson or two," added the other. Their nervous tension gave way to relief, and their comments were correspondingly smug. "Now, let's make this handoff nice and quick, yeah?"

However, when the two knights demanded that Shura give them the High School Prodigies...

"No."

...she coldly refused.

"Huh?"

"I need the grandmaster to promise never to interfere with Yamato's affairs again before I relinquish them. Until then, I won't let you lay a finger on the captives."

"You little punk, you think this is a game or someth—?"

"Not in the slightest."

"…"

Shura didn't falter in the face of a military group thirty thousand strong. That was menacing on its own to the pair of Gold Knights. As the two of them recoiled in awe, Shura went on. "We did what you asked. Now it's your turn to show some sincerity. If you give me any more lip, you're not getting them. And if you try seizing them by force, I'll cut you all down."

"H…ha-ha! Looks like the White Wolf General's got some fight in her!"

"Sh-she's so overconfident that it's actually hilarious!"

A single girl stood before thirty thousand soldiers, threatening to slay them. The whole thing was preposterous. The knights and soldiers laughed, guffawing with great smiles. However, their grins froze tight on their faces only moments after.

The truth dawned on them.

Sure, there was no way she could actually kill thirty thousand troops on her own. But the thing was…Shura was Yamato's samurai general, and her combat prowess was unrivaled. Even if she couldn't fell the whole group, the three hundred or so nearest to her would undoubtedly die.

"Fine. We'll take you to the grandmaster."

"But in exchange, you have to let us surround you. And don't even *think* of pulling any funny business."

The two knights reluctantly accepted Shura's demand and allowed her into their encampment.

It was negligent of them. Careless. But who could blame them for the decision? Shura wouldn't attack thirty thousand soldiers alone. Her threat was a mere bluff. Even if she died a hero's death and claimed three hundred on her way out, it wouldn't change the greater war situation. She would die for nothing.

Why would a warrior about to become Yamato's samurai general choose such a meaningless death? She wouldn't. It was unthinkable.

And that was precisely why her surprise attack was guaranteed to work.

"Mwa-ha-ha. Now then, kiddos, allow me to reveal the truth! The item you've chosen…is sugar!"

"Whaaaaat?!?!"

"But how did you know?!"

"How? Bwa-ha-ha! Reading your tiny minds is child's play for one so omnipotent!"

"Whooooa!"

"You're amazing, God Akatsuki!"

"But that's so unscientific…"

While the High School Prodigies were seemingly away, about to get handed over to the imperial army, Prince Akatsuki was looking after some children in Azuchi, entertaining them with simple magic tricks.

"Thank you so much for helping out, Akatsuki," said Lyrule, who was serving as his assistant.

"What, the kids? Of course. This stuff is easy peasy." Akatsuki looked up at the moonless sky. "Tsukasa and the others must be getting started about now."

Suddenly, the blood drained from Lyrule's face. "…"

"Is everything okay?"

"He saw… Tsukasa saw…everything… Ohhh…," she mumbled. She trembled, and as the quivering intensified…

"UGH!"

...she eventually exploded in rage.

"I can't believe her, I can't believe her, I can't believe her! Yggdra, you jerk! You jerky jerkface! If you think I'll ever let you possess me again after that, you can think again, missy! And in front of Tsukasa, no less... Oh, I can't. I can't! I just caaaaaaan't!"

Lyrule, face bright red, sobbed as she recalled the humiliation she'd suffered while unconscious back at the elf village.

"H-hey, don't worry about it. Tsukasa gave her his jacket right away."

"That's not the issue!"

Akatsuki understood Lyrule's feelings. During his time in elementary school, he was picked on for his looks, and he still recalled the misery from when a classmate pulled down his pants and underwear. It had brought him to tears then, and Akatsuki could imagine how much worse it felt for a teenager.

Tsukasa surely sympathized, thus...

"Seriously, you don't have to worry. Tsukasa would never commit to memory something that makes you uncomfortable. He's probably already purged the image from his mind!"

...Akatsuki tried to use that to cheer Lyrule up.

However, a conflicted expression crossed the girl's face...

"Th-that would make me sad, too, in its own way..."

"Huh?"

"N-n-n-n-nothing!"

...and she pursed her lips and whispered something Akatsuki couldn't make out.

The magician tilted his head in confusion.

Before he had a chance to ask follow-up questions, though...

"Hey! Hey, God!"

...a group of bandaged Yamato soldiers came rushing over to him.

©Sacraneco

There were twenty in all.

"Wh-wha-what's going on?! Errr, what cause have you for this commotion, mortals?" Akatsuki asked, choking back his surprise. The soldiers surrounding him were among those injured in the recent battle. They flung questions at him with frantic looks in their eyes.

"Is it true that Shura's team left for the front already?!"

"What the hell?! Why didn't they bring us along?!"

"Yeah, I don't get it! A broken bone or two is a scratch for a Yamato samurai! We can still fight!"

"I-I'm sure that, uh…," Akatsuki stammered.

Blood trickled from the bandages wrapped around the soldiers' foreheads, yet they demanded to know why they weren't called to battle. As they lamented that their friends had departed without them, Akatsuki found himself at a loss for words.

However…

"I'm afraid none of you is fit to go."

…the prodigy doctor Keine Kanzaki came over in her white doctor's coat when she saw the wounded soldiers kicking up a fuss and chided them in Akatsuki's place.

"Keine?"

"Ms. Angel Doctor…"

"Anyone who isn't in *tip-top shape* will jeopardize the operation," Keine said. "Your sole job is to rest."

"B-but they're up against thirty thousand soldiers!"

"They need all the help they can get, even from the wounded!"

Keine shook her head. "Another one hundred and twenty thousand soldiers are waiting behind those thirty. This battle will be a skirmish, nothing more. Pushing yourselves and aggravating your injuries now would leave you unfit for when a truly decisive battle arrives. Besides, there are young children here who need looking after."

"I mean…"

"…"

The coming conflict was going to be an all-out war between Yamato and Freyjagard, and everyone knew it. The soldiers had no choice but to surrender to Keine's logic. Even if they understood it in their heads, though, their hearts were a different matter. Sitting back and relaxing while allies stood against a huge disadvantage felt wrong. Their expressions darkened with guilt.

If they kept on like that, it was likely to affect their recoveries. That was a problem, as their sole job right now was to heal up as fast as possible so they'd be ready to fight in the future.

To put her patients at ease, Keine gave a relaxed smile…

"I understand the concern over the enemy's numbers. However, I ask that you do your best to trust our allies. There's no need to worry. After all, I know Aoi's strength better than anyone."

…and looked to the western sky, toward where the hero she'd worked beside for so long was fighting.

"I would say that Aoi is worth a thousand soldiers, *but I'm afraid that would be selling her short.*"

While Keine voiced her faith in Aoi Ichijou…

"Shall we begin?"

…that very same prodigy swordmaster, who'd been brought to the enemy camp, ripped through her shackles like they were made of dead branches.

"Huh?"

The imperial knights' eyes went wide at the shocking turn of events.

Naturally, Aoi had no intention of giving them time to get their bearings.

"Shura, m'lady!"

"On it."

Shura removed Mikazuki's lapis lazuli sheath from her waist and tossed it over. Aoi caught it and drew the blade faster than the eye could see, cutting away her fellow prisoners' shackles.

"Arrrrrgh!"

Her stroke caught a few of the enemy soldiers, too.

Finally, the knights were making sense of the situation. "I-it was a setup! Those Yamato bastards betrayed us!" they shouted.

To that, the newly freed Shinobu Sarutobi...

"Not much of a betrayal if we were on opposite sides from the start!"

...picked up one of the fallen soldiers' swords and slashed at the Gold Knights' throats.

That's right, Shinobu Sarutobi. The one who'd left to go on a solo mission in the empire. She shouldn't have been there. And it wasn't just her, either. Tsukasa, Ringo, and even Akatsuki cleaved through the imperial troops with masterful swordplay. None of it made any sense—or rather, it wouldn't have if it were truly them.

Aoi Ichijou was the only genuine High School Prodigy among their ranks. All the others were Yamato ninjas. By disguising themselves, they'd fooled their enemies into dropping their guards.

"You all have weapons now, I trust?" Aoi asked.

"That we do, Ms. Angel!"

"They're not the greatest, but they're plenty for us to smash in these weak little bean sprouts' heads!"

Aoi nodded. "Then let us be off!"

"All units, scatter!" Shura barked.

"""Yes, ma'am!"""

On Shura's command, the Yamato ninjas in the imperial vanguard headquarters let out a battle cry and turned their weapons on the horrified Freyjagard infantry.

"What the hell?!" an imperial exclaimed. "Nobody in their right mind would storm an enemy camp with a squad that small!"

"Ha!" one of the ninjas laughed. "Anyone from Yamato would gladly lay down their life for their nation. That's even true of royal family members! You think this is enough to make a ninja lose heart?!"

"Arrrrgh!"

"They're too strong!"

"Use your heads, you idiots! I don't care if they're from Yamato; we still have them surrounded! Just crush them with numbers! Box each of them in and beat them dead!"

As Aoi and the ninjas charged the enemy line and mowed their way through the enemy camp, their opponents panicked. The imperial knights shouted angrily at their cowardly subordinates, and the fact of the matter was, they were right. Yamato warriors were unmistakably strong, but each was a match for only ten Freyjagard soldiers at most. The imperials' current numbers advantage far surpassed ten-to-one. All they had to do was throw more bodies at the ninjas than they could handle.

It was the perfect plan.

Or it would have been if not for the new moon.

"Agh! Quit shoving me, you dumbass!"

"I—I can't! We're packed in too tight!"

"Where'd they go?! It's too dark to see any— URK!"

"These bastards are using the cover of night to blend in with the crowd!"

Torches didn't shed light very far, and the visibility problem worsened with so many people packed together. Catching the Yamato ninjas weaving through the ranks was impossible.

And to make matters worse...

"Damn it; they're just killing everyone within reach!"

...the numbers advantage that would usually have given the empire the edge was working against it.

Each of the imperial soldiers was surrounded by friendlies. They wanted to avoid hitting their allies in the dark, and that stayed their sword arms.

For the Yamato ninjas, though, it was the exact opposite. Being so thoroughly outnumbered allowed them to cut down others indiscriminately without concern they might hit an ally. They could lash out at any humanoid shape in the dark with impunity, and they did just that, cleaving through all obstructions while utterly unimpeded by the night.

It quickly dawned on the knights how much danger they were in. They shouted new orders to get the troops to move apart. "Clumping up like this is just playing into their hands! Fall back and spread out for now! Spread ooooout!"

However, it was too late.

The ninjas smirked. "Ha! You really think we'll let you off the hook that easily?!"

They'd deftly turned the whole situation to their advantage, but they numbered only a handful. Once the Freyjagard side rallied and took advantage of its size, the ninjas would be overrun immediately. Not even Yamato soldiers could keep on fighting forever.

So why had they sprung this bold raid with so few? How could they fight a suicidal battle with such glee?

The answer was simple.

The surprise attack was a diversion to ensure the real ambush was successful.

""AAAAAAGH!!!!"""
"Wh-what's going on?!"

An abrupt chorus of screams sounded from across the hill like thunder. And as the bewildered soldiers braced themselves...

"I-it's an ambush! Those Yamato bastards are charging out from the woods!"

"They used the others as a distraction to get in close! W-we're surrounded!"

...news of the real situation arrived.

A war cry shook the night.

""""HRAAAAAAAAH!"""""

"We can't let our samurai general hog *all* the glory!"

"Mow them down, every one of 'em!"

Approximately a thousand soldiers from the main Yamato Army came pouring from the woods around the hill, carving their way through bunched-up imperial warriors just as Aoi and the ninjas had.

As Aoi observed...

The plan gave me pause when first I heard it, but I never imagined they would fall so thoroughly for our ploy!

...she offered silent thanks to the one who'd proposed this brilliant tactic.

"You wouldst have us take the initiative, then?"

"That's right."

After receiving the message from Foremost and rushing back to Yamato, Tsukasa held a meeting with Kaguya about how to respond. He proposed making the first move instead of waiting for Freyjagard.

"There's no room for negotiation on our end, so one way or another, this war is happening. Trying to avoid the inevitable will weaken our position. We should launch a surprise attack while the enemy still thinks they can bait us into bargaining and try to do enough damage to improve our tactical situation."

"I must say, I'd not taken you for such a warmonger."

"I like to think of it as proactive self-defense."

That earned a chuckle out of Kaguya. "Ah, what a way you have with words." Her expression swiftly turned serious again. "I am of a mind to adopt this plan of yours. The question is, how do we accomplish it?"

Tsukasa laid out the specifics. "We start with the thirty thousand camped out on that hill by the border. We'll pretend to accept their terms to get close, then have Aoi, Shura, and a few other capable fighters strike. That'll throw the enemy vanguard into chaos. Then, before our enemies can collect themselves, our main force will rush the flanks...

"...surrounding and exterminating thirty thousand troops with only a thousand from Yamato."

"Wh—?!" Kaguya's eyes went wide. Tsukasa had suggested they encircle thirty thousand enemies with a mere thousand of their own troops. She thought it had to be a joke.

However, Tsukasa was serious.

"The plan seems terrible if you only consider the numbers, of course, but the people of Yamato have physical abilities that far outstrip the imperials'. The last war with Freyjagard was primarily conducted with orderly group clashes, but this will be a chaotic close-quarters skirmish with both sides jumbled together. Orders won't travel well. It's the perfect opportunity for individually capable warriors to shine."

The numerical disadvantage wouldn't change, and Yamato couldn't win this war through conventional means. It needed to flip things around such that battles weren't about total size but the individuals engaged. As Tsukasa explained, that was the only way they were going to be able to survive.

Kaguya seemed hesitant at first...

"I think it's a good idea."

...but Shura, who was attending the war council as Yamato's new samurai general, approved of the plan.

"If anything, this is how we've always fought."

Guerrilla tactics were one of the best ways to take advantage of capable lone warriors. During the last Yamato war, that was one of the big reasons that the nation had held off Freyjagard's huge force for months despite Mayoi's betrayal causing catastrophic losses during the first few days of the conflict.

Upon hearing the confidence in Shura's voice, Kaguya steeled her resolve in turn. "Very well. If my samurai general says it's possible, that is proof enough for me."

Shura nodded. "Mm."

With that, the strategy was decided.

Tsukasa turned from Kaguya to Shura, the person in charge of managing Yamato's armed forces. "We'll carry out the operation just before the deadline Neuro set for your response, on the night of the new moon in seven days.

"Our mission is simple: advance and annihilate. When the time comes, don't worry whether the person before you is an enemy. Don't think. Don't make decisions. Thinking gives your opponents a chance. And when you're cornered on all sides, an opening could prove fatal.

"If you have time to think, you have time to slash. If there's a moment to make a decision, it should be spent wielding your blade. There'll be hostiles every way you look. Focus on cleaving through every person you can reach. Anything less means you won't get out alive. Make sure your soldiers understand that."

Shura gave Tsukasa a resolute nod.

The new moon was a supreme stroke of good fortune for the Yamato side, allowing Tsukasa's unusual night raid to go off without a hitch.

The samurai knew their homeland like the backs of their hands. When Aoi's group sprang the surprise attack and scattered the imperial vanguard, the Yamato forces encircled them immediately. From there, all the samurai had to do was press inward. They charged their huddled foes, taking full advantage of their natural talents.

By contrast...

"Hey! Quit shoving me, asshole!"

"What the hell are you guys doing?! Just kill them already!"

"AAARGH! We're on the same side, dammit!"

"I can't even tell what's going on! Where are the hostiles?!"

"A-ahhhhh! I—I can't take this anymore! I wanna go hooooome!"

…the imperial soldiers succumbed to terror and were thoroughly routed.

Their huge numbers were backfiring in a big way.

With no moon and the torchlight blocked by the mob, they couldn't see the oncoming Yamato warriors. Spurred by terror, the imperials accidentally struck one another. The knights at the center of the imperial ranks couldn't bear to stand around doing nothing, and while they wished to rush in to provide backup…

"Shit, shit, shit! Even if we try to help, there are too many friendlies for us to swing our swords!"

"And while we're busy tripping over one another, the enemies are free to cleave through our ranks! Grouping up makes us sitting ducks!"

"We've gotta fix our visibility problem! That means more light! I want Dragon Knights in the sky over every spot we're being attacked! Go, go, go!"

…things were too chaotic for that. So they settled for barking new orders.

The Dragon Knights hurriedly paired with mages and prepared for takeoff. The plan was to take the mages up and have them spread light all across the battlefield.

That was the standard operating procedure for fighting nighttime battles. And because it was the typical strategy, the Yamato side knew how to respond.

"There's…movement…at the back…of the enemy lines."

"Can you be more specific, Ringo?"

"Um… It looks like…they're getting their dragons…flight ready."

"Good. That's what we expected."

Over in the woods near the battle, Tsukasa and Ringo waited in their truck and watched the imperials via a satellite flying high above the ground.

They had no intention of letting their enemies do as they pleased. The two had preparations in place to dash the imperials' hopes.

"It's our job to provide the backup. Let's do this," Tsukasa said.

Ringo nodded. "Bearabbit, *start the engine.*"

"*Pawger that!*"

On Ringo's order, the entire truck shook.

Meanwhile, over at the imperial vanguard encampment...

"Those damn samurai bumpkins think they're all that. We'll see who's laughing now!"

"You mages charge steep rates for your services. It's time for you to earn your keep."

"From what I hear, you Dragon Knights earn a fair amount, too."

Yamato's attacks hadn't reached the center of the imperial camp, so things there remained relatively calm. Once each Dragon Knight had a mage seated behind them, they all took off into the moonless dark.

As their allies below scattered like rats in the face of the Yamato offensive...

"*Lightbolt.*"

...the mages lit up the sky with what looked like miniature suns.

The lights were blinding up close, but they perfectly illuminated the surroundings for those on the ground. Powerful beams of white light seared their way across the night, revealing their foes.

"There they are! Surround them!"

"Ah!"

"Arrrrgh!"

With the Yamato fighters visible, they'd lost their advantage. A single Yamato samurai could hold their own against ten soldiers, but the imperials could easily provide twenty for a single opponent. The light had exposed the Yamato soldiers, and the imperials began overpowering them with their numbers.

The Dragon Knights cheered as they flew back and forth to brighten the sky with magical light. Yamato's strategy relied on hiding in darkness, and the Dragon Knights were glad to rob them of it. With the sky illuminated, Yamato's battle plan would collapse.

However...

...Tsukasa had prepared for this.

"Huh?"

The Dragon Knights came to a halt in midair. They were a fair distance above the clash on the ground, so they could recognize something was happening in the distance. An unsettling noise was rumbling from somewhere nearby, a sound like a repeated explosion. And it was getting closer.

"What's up with that noise?"

"H-hey, what the hell is that thing?!"

The cacophony grew steadily greater, and when the Dragon Knights followed the noise to its origin, they spotted something over Azuchi. It gave off a bizarre chopping noise, as though rending the air. Once it got closer, the knights realized it was a flying object with a pair of lights.

"They've got a dragon?! No, wait, it looks like it's made of *bone* or something. I've never seen anything like it!"

"Why are its eyes glowing like that?!"

The object was about sixteen hundred feet away now, and the Dragon Knights gawked as they stared into their spyglasses with shock. Between the shafts of light coming from its eyes and its hard exterior, the approaching object wasn't even clearly a living being.

The Dragon Knights' confusion was understandable. The people of this world lacked the knowledge to comprehend the approaching machine. Ringo Oohoshi had taken the frame and engine from the Prodigies' truck and attached a propeller on top, while Bearabbit had handled the electronics manually. The result was a makeshift helicopter.

"Agh! Wh-what's going on?!"

"Something just came shooting out of the bone dragon!"

A massive roar shook the air like thunder, even overpowering the helicopter blades. A scarlet streak shot from the helicopter, rocketing past the Dragon Knights.

One incomprehensible thing happened after another, and the Dragon Knights lacked the capacity to process it all.

That said, it took little time for them to understand the danger they were in.

"Aaagh!"

"Gyaaah!"

Ruptures burst in succession. With each one, a Dragon Knight fell, all of them spraying blood as they dropped lifelessly from the sky.

One knight's head was blown clean off. Another's dragon lost a wing. The source of the booms was...

"A sniper! Whoever's riding that bone dragon thing is shooting us!"

"D-don't be crazy—we're sixteen hundred feet from that thing! What the hell kind of gun can land hits from tha—? GAH!"

With each flash, another crimson flower bloomed in the sky.

Thanks to its night-vision scope, the sniper rifle was able to strike down the imperials' air support with terrifying precision. Bearabbit had borrowed one of Yamato's wrought iron forges to cobble it together, and the person pulling the trigger...

"Ten down."

...was none other than prodigy politician Tsukasa Mikogami.

"Th-that's amazing, Tsuclawsa! Are you sure you're not secretly a pawdigy marksman?"

"Any *real* prodigy marksman would have landed that first shot, too. The whole point of sniping is to exact certain death. Missing my first round makes me third-rate at best." Tsukasa shrugged. He was no virtuoso, that was for sure. "Still, even a dabbler has his place—and right now, mine is here."

As he spoke, Tsukasa pulled the breechblock on the rifle he'd brought from Elm and ejected the spent shell. Then he steadied the gunstock against his shoulder, took aim...

...and fired.

With every pull of the trigger, another dragon Tsukasa spied through his night-vision scope dropped to the ground like a stone.

Tsukasa's movements were as fluid as a running stream. There wasn't so much as an ounce of hesitation to his shots because there was no need to be. The reason for that lay in his first shot—the one he'd described as a miss. It had flown past the Dragon Knights, painting a red trail through the dark; the special bullet was called a tracer round. By watching the arc it drew through the air, Tsukasa had discerned the effect his rifle, the crosswind, and the helicopter's shaking had on his shots. Armed with that information, all that remained was to find the right position, take aim, and fire.

It took a lot of work to pull a trigger without letting the

barrel shake, but Tsukasa had training. If a result could be achieved through hard work, *Tsukasa always made sure to put in the hours.*

"Twenty down."

Tsukasa Mikogami wasn't a prodigy. Not the sort he'd referred to, at least. When any of the other High School Prodigies learned something new in their field of expertise, they could use that one fact to comprehend ten more, then put those ten to a hundred different uses. But not Tsukasa. Whenever he learned something, it remained singular, no matter the subject in question. He could even be called the archetypical everyman.

However, *he learned that fact down to his bones.*

Whenever Tsukasa took something in, he spared no effort in comprehending it entirely, making it a part of himself. That ideology underpinned everything Tsukasa Mikogami did—his uncompromising focus and devotion. His methods weren't limited to political work. That was how he approached everything. His old friend Masato Sanada had described him thusly:

"Tsukasa Mikogami might never become the best at anything. But the thing is, he can be the second best at everything."

"Fifty."

Tsukasa had felled a third of the Dragon Knights, and that hadn't gone unnoticed. The Dragon Knights realized they'd be of no use to their allies below until they handled this new threat.

"Dammit, they're picking us off like flies!"

"We have to stop that bone dragon!"

"HRAAAAAAAAH!!!!"

The one-sided, long-range massacre sparked a fury in the

Dragon Knights that roared like an inferno. They bellowed with rage as their dragons soared, beelining for Tsukasa's helicopter as fast as they could.

There were more than a hundred of them, and not even Tsukasa could drop that many knights when they came charging at once. A single rifle couldn't fire that many shots in time, even if every bullet found its mark. And while the helicopter did have a Gatling gun left over from its former life as a truck, the weapon's accuracy couldn't hold a candle to Tsukasa's sniper rifle, making it a poor deterrent against the coming horde.

Like it or not, the knights were closing in.

Once the dragons got within three hundred feet, the helicopter would fall under the mages' firing range. There was no way a makeshift copter would withstand a concentrated magical bombardment from all directions.

Yet...the Dragon Knights' attack proved foolish.

Flying over a forest in enemy territory was like begging to be killed.

"A-agh! There are arrows coming out of the forest!"

"Yamato soldiers! They've got archers down there!"

Fire arrows came speeding up at the Dragon Knights from the woods. On Tsukasa's instructions, Hibari's archer squad had remained hidden in the trees instead of joining the battle at the onset. Waiting under the Dragon Knights' projected flight path gave them the perfect position to shoot them down.

The fire arrows found their marks in the dragons' wings and chests, and the creatures shrieked as they faltered and tumbled in droves, disappearing into the forest canopy.

Losing their allies dramatically curbed the remaining Dragon

Knights' enthusiasm. And when they slowed their charge…they became easier targets.

""""AHHHHHHHHHH!!!!""""

Tsukasa took aim and used his keen accuracy to shoot them down one by one.

If the imperials acted decisively and continued their push, ignoring the arrows, the fight might have turned in their favor. Hidden archers were a problem, but felling a dragon in flight from directly below wasn't easy. Most of the Dragon Knights would have survived, yet they'd stopped.

Why?

It was because of Tsukasa's decision to specifically employ *fire* arrows.

Fire arrows were deadly projectiles capable of inflicting wounds via the piercing tips or the intense flames. However, they also revealed where the archers were, defeating the point of attacking under the cover of night. The Dragon Knights would've had a much harder time evading if the arrows weren't alight.

So why bother using them? Because Tsukasa *wanted* the imperials to see.

A massive volley of burning spikes was a terrifying image. Arrows could fly wide of the Dragon Knights' bodies, but they'd strike their hearts regardless. Fear would cause the riders to falter, and their courage would fail.

Tsukasa knew that the moment the Dragon Knights lost their nerve, their fates were sealed.

"One hundred down. I think that about does it."

The imperial vanguard's air unit fell for Tsukasa's anti–Dragon Knight strategy completely. Between him, Hibari's squad, and Bearabbit's machine gunning, the aerial threat was completely neutralized.

With the airspace now fully under the Yamato side's control…

"Now that we've cleaned up their pesky fleet, I'd say it's time we pressed onward. Set a course for the middle of the enemy's camp."

"You…got it…!"

…Tsukasa took the opportunity to have the helicopter continue ahead.

What followed could hardly be described as a battle.

After demolishing the Dragon Knights, the helicopter made its way over to the imperial ground forces. The soldiers had never seen anything like it before, but between its bizarre appearance and horrible roar, they quickly descended into panic. And when the machine gun fire started, that chaos worsened. The sixty hunks of lead the helicopter was able to pump out each second mowed through the imperial vanguard.

Some of the soldiers were brave enough to gather mages and riflemen, hoping to mount a counteroffensive, but Ringo's satellite saw right through that effort, and Tsukasa made short work of the ralliers with his sniper rifle. Ultimately, the imperials' formation crumbled, and the soldiers fled. They had ceased to be a functional military unit.

However, even retreating was no easy feat. The Yamato samurai were still rampaging all across the camp's perimeter, and when the helicopter's assault scattered the soldiers in the center, it put even more pressure on those engaged with the samurai. When the two sets of imperials crashed into each other, they suffered more friendly fire than ever.

The situation tipped further in Yamato's favor by the moment. Each samurai was like a legion unto themselves, and their rank of a meager one thousand encircled and exterminated the thirty thousand from Freyjagard in earnest. The imperials had lost their will to fight, and the Yamato soldiers stained the meadowed hill with dark blood as they shot and sliced their way through.

Ringo's heart felt like it was going to tear itself in two as she watched.

However...

"..."

...she continued aiding Tsukasa.

Whenever the Freyjagard forces tried to rally or run, she reported it so the Yamato troops could annihilate them efficiently.

She did it because Tsukasa had told her to.

No, she wasn't just blindly following his orders. She did it because she knew. When people came looking to hurt you, mercy wasn't an option. You couldn't hesitate to strike back.

To date, Ringo had been the subject of 172 kidnapping attempts and 115 assassination plots. One of the former even succeeded.

There were people far crueler than Ringo could imagine. Some were willing to inflict any amount of pain on others if it meant securing their own happiness.

And Ringo understood that her hesitation could prove fatal. The enemies numbered thirty thousand. Freyjagard had every intention of cruelly murdering Yamato's troops with their thirty-to-one advantage. Wanton hostility begets no wavering. Ringo knew that. Occasionally, the only recourse to violence wielded for unjust ends was to respond in kind.

If you weren't willing to fight when it mattered, then you couldn't save anything.

You couldn't save yourself or those dear to you.

Being weak wasn't a sin, but using it as an excuse to do nothing definitely was.

* * *

The dying soldiers were likely guilty only of blindly following Neuro.

However, Ringo had decided not to falter.

Only a saint willingly laid down their life for a stranger, and Ringo was no saint.

"Analysis complete. My satellite has…the locations…of every ally…on the battlefield."

She completed her assigned task, fully aware of the consequences.

"I appreciate it," Tsukasa replied. He was thanking her from the heart for everything—both for how conflicted she was and for her determination. "Now, target every area where the hostiles are grouped up and commence the bombing."

This air raid would end things.

Ringo's satellite imagery provided the precise locations of those allies who'd infiltrated the enemy camp. Bombs rained from the helicopter, bound for spots where they wouldn't harm friendlies. There hadn't been sufficient time to manufacture new explosives, so the payloads were grenades left over from the war against the dominion government. Fortunately, the imperials were so bunched up that the blasts managed to inflict serious damage. Each grenade caught as many as ten soldiers.

Tsukasa used the term *"annihilate"* back in the briefing, and the helicopter's merciless attack was well worthy of the word.

Barely thirty minutes had passed since the fighting began. In that time, Yamato had suffered less than thirty losses, whereas the empire's were well over a thousand.

At that point, Tsukasa got a call from Aoi.

"The enemy vanguard is largely beaten. Naught surrounds me but corpses. What would you have me do now, m'lord?"

They'd already achieved a solid victory, and Aoi was asking if Tsukasa wished for her to fall back.

Tsukasa replied without a moment's hesitation. "Looking at the situation, we've already dealt our opponents more than a thousand casualties. Considering the size of their army, though, it's far from a decisive blow. For the entirety of the war, this will likely be our only time to go on the offensive. We need to take full advantage of the opportunity to instill fear of us and Yamato in our foes to ensure the skirmishes to come are skewed in our favor."

If Yamato got stuck in a protracted defensive war, it wouldn't be long before Elm took action. Tsukasa had been informed of the election results and that the government had members from the Principles Party and Reform Party alike. However Elm decided to approach the situation, Tsukasa was confident they'd aid Yamato.

And if Yamato wished to stall until Elm got involved…

"It's time for us to push ourselves to the limit and take everything we can."

"So…"

"We continue advancing and annihilating. Our aerial bombing has our foes' ranks in chaos, and I need your group to charge them from the rear. Meanwhile, we'll keep hitting them from the sky. I feel a little bad for the imperial troops…but I need them all dead—tonight."

"…Very well!"

As the imperial army continued collapsing, the Yamato forces pressed the attack even harder, gunning their foes down as they fled.

Despite the advantage, Tsukasa's expression remained tense.

The surprise attack proved wildly successful, and his side was winning, but he knew that today's accomplishments amounted to little. A loss of a thousand troops wouldn't affect Freyjagard's staggering numbers. If the Yamato forces offered the slightest chance to recover, the tides would shift immediately, and the imperials would crush the samurai.

Freyjagard had nearly every advantage conceivable. This was no time for Tsukasa to relax or let his guard down.

Armed with data from Ringo's satellite, Tsukasa monitored the enemy's movements, watching for any organized efforts. When he spotted one, he nipped it in the bud with an air raid before the cohesion spread to the rest of the army.

To win—to survive—Tsukasa had to take the best option at every junction. But even after making so many correct moves…

"…"

…he was more worried than ever about the person in command of those unfortunate soldiers.

The true foe operated outside this world's rules, much as the Prodigies did. Things wouldn't continue as Tsukasa deigned forever. He understood that, and it gave him a feeling like dryness in the back of his throat. Soon, the seemingly perfect strategy would fail.

Before long, his hunch would come to pass in the worst possible way.

"Yeesh. I gotta hand it to that Tsukasa; those are some cold-blooded moves."

The dazzlingly grand imperial castle set in Freyjagard's capital, Drachen, stood as a symbol of the empire itself. The nobles' district surrounded the palace on all sides, and the military headquarters within that section of the city were the beating heart of the nation's armed forces.

Currently, a war council was gathered in the headquarters, deliberating on the Yamato matter. The country overthrew Freyjagard's dominion government and redeclared independence the other day. What's more, the Seven Luminaries aided the revolt.

Sitting at the head of the table was the man who summoned the empire's lords, Blue Grandmaster Neuro ul Levias. He heaved an exasperated sigh. "Do I seriously have to try against these apes? Honestly, I'd prefer not to."

His gaze rested upon the center of the room's round table. There was a large crystal ball affixed there, and its surface displayed an image of the battle at the Yamato border. Neuro's magic allowed him to project an image from soldiers' eyes to monitor the conflict in real time.

The scene had the gathered lords agitated. "Blue Grandmaster, why aren't you taking this more seriously?!" one exclaimed, admonishing Neuro for his nonchalance.

"I can't believe they actually chose to attack *us*," another lord added. "We have thirty thousand troops, for crying out loud!"

"Yeah, I assumed they'd remain holed up in their fortresses. They completely caught us off guard."

"Grandmaster, do you have some sort of plan?!"

Freyjagard's thirty thousand soldiers were being overpowered by a mere thousand. Even after accounting for the powerful dragon aiding the Yamato side, the result was still unthinkable. None of the elderly nobles knew what to make of the events.

Neuro was the person in charge, so they naturally heaped blame on him and demanded he provide a solution.

Of all the people in the council room, though...

"A plan? Why would I need a plan? I really don't understand why you all seem so alarmed."

...Neuro was the one whose composure remained relaxed.

No, *"composure"* didn't capture it. He was *confident*.

Neuro leaned back in his chair as though to say that there was nothing worth fretting about. "Oh, sure, this is a nasty attack. They've got the geographic advantage, those Yamato soldiers who specialize in solo combat, and the support to ensure we can't fight back. If things continue like this, it's only a matter of time before we lose all thirty thousand of our men."

"I-if you understand that much, then why—?"

"Because things *can't* continue like this."

"Huh?"

"Isn't it obvious? A person only has so much stamina. Not even the people of Yamato, *the descendants of test subjects*, can go on endlessly. They fight in peak condition for now, but that will break."

"Test subjects...?"

"Actually, he has a point."

"Yeah, now that he mentions it..."

"In an hour, exhaustion will eat at them, and we'll rally our forces and crush them with our numbers," Neuro declared. "Even if that's enough time to kill a full half of the force at the encampment, it will still leave us with fifteen thousand troops. A thousand soldiers was never enough to win against thirty thousand. No matter the world, that's impossible."

There were a few things the aristocrats didn't understand, but Neuro's reasoning was solid. He was right—Yamato wouldn't win. Not even the peerless samurai could pull victory from such an overwhelming disadvantage. Eliminating all the imperial troops was never a realistic plan.

"Knowing that, I imagine our opponents won't dare press their luck. They came at us hard to whip up their soldiers' morale, but… the young man who engineered this situation is a clever sort. After whittling away as many of our soldiers as he can safely, I'm certain he'll withdraw."

This was the only chance Yamato had to spring a successful surprise attack, so it had chosen to reject Freyjagard's demands in favor of claiming an advantage for the battles to come.

In short, Neuro's foes were choosing a sort of proactive conservationist tactic.

Hiding in fortresses would end poorly for the Yamato forces, as would suicide attacks as a show of defiance. Instead, they chose the long game, using surprise aggression to chip away at the imperials' strength.

It was a clear declaration that Yamato desired to win this war.

Neuro let out a dry chuckle. "Seriously, what did I do to deserve such hatred? Yggdra's the one who dragged them into this world, so are they siding with *her*? I swear, I'll never understand what makes apes tick."

"…Blue Grandmaster?"

"Don't mind me—just talking to myself." Neuro waved off the ignorant nobles as one would buzzing flies, then stood from his chair. "Any move we try to cobble together now will be too late, and letting those schemers get one over on us will boost their spirits. If they want to play the long game, then we'll do the same. And since that's the plan…we need to start by crushing those eyes of theirs."

"Their…eyes? Do they have magic like yours that lets them see through the eyes of others?"

"No," Neuro replied, "they have something nastier. They're

watching the whole battlefield from a vantage point beyond the clouds. That's how they keep stamping out our soldiers the moment they regroup!"

"You mean that thing from the rumors, then—God Akatsuki's all-seeing clairvoyance!"

"If that's real, then it's no wonder they keep countering our flanking maneuvers and surprise attacks!"

Neuro nodded. "Exactly. It hardly seems fair. That's why those eyes have gotta go."

"D-do you know some way to do that?"

The older gentlemen stared pleadingly at Neuro, who gave them a smile…

"I do indeed. That's why I had you bring *them* here."

…and pushed open the council room's hefty double doors. They were ornamented with gold, silver, and jade, and they creaked under their own weight as they moved. Beyond was a wide plaza where soldiers trained. However, no knights walked the yard at the moment.

Instead, a group of people was chained to a stake, their faces illuminated by a bonfire. All were handsomely dressed, and their skin and hair were well cared for. These were no commoners. They were nobles: namely, the Bluebloods who'd tried to overthrow the Lindworm regime.

"And hello there to you, my Blueblood friends!" Neuro greeted. "Terribly sorry for making you wait in the cold like that."

Upon seeing the man who held their fates in his hand, the roughly five hundred prisoners shouted and begged.

"B-Blue Grandmaster!"

"Please d-don't kill us! Weltenbruger's the one who led us astray. He tricked us!"

"You have to spare my family. At least show mercy for my daughter!"

"W-we're Freyjagard nobles, in case you've forgotten. You really think some upstart like you has the right to treat us this way?! Release us at once!"

"Mommy! I want my mommy!"

Neuro replied...

"Ha-ha-ha. I'm glad to see you're all in such high spirits. You're a hearty bunch; I'll give you that much."

...with a nod and a satisfied smile.

"And that's what makes us such good teammates."

"Team...mates?"

That was perhaps the last word the nobles had expected to hear from Neuro, and they stopped their pleading, hopeful for what he might say next.

"That's right. We're all allies in serving the Freyjagard Empire. Sure, you started a little insurrection, but I can tell you only did so out of love for your country. I'm an open-minded-enough guy to appreciate that."

"Y-yeah, you're right! That's exactly what it was, Mr. Grandmaster!"

"You're a wise man, Blue Grandmaster, and you have a discerning eye for character!"

The Bluebloods and their relatives couldn't have imagined a more fortuitous turn of events. Neuro's amiable attitude earned him favor-currying smiles from every prisoner.

However...

"That I do. Your patriotism moves me. So now...let's you and I destroy together those who would harm the empire!"

...those smiles soon vanished.

The moment Neuro tapped his staff against the ground, a massive white magic circle formed, covering the entire plaza.

* * *

""""ARRRRRRRRRRRRRRRGH!!!!""""

Five hundred screams shook the Drachen sky.

"It bur... IT BUUUURNS!!"

"What're these stones? They're clinging to my bod-bod—AHHHHHHH!!"

"Gah-gahgahgah-GLURGH!!"

The chained-up nobles writhed like worms. Each had a necklace draped around their neck when brought here. The black crystals on them emitted terrible heat and melted into the nobles' chests. The dark gems—Father's cells—were rewriting the organic material around them, transforming it.

The nobles were evolving, whether they wanted to or not.

Anyone implanted with Father's cells was changed. Black crystals sprouted from the victims' bodies, tearing through flesh and crushing bones as they propagated. The nobles were no longer human beings. They'd been reduced to grotesque porcupines.

And it wasn't just the Bluebloods who changed...

"Ahhhhhh!!"

...the same occurred to the nobles standing beside Neuro as well. They screamed in confusion as their flesh tore from the inside out.

"B-but, Grandmaster, wh-WHYYYYYYY?!?!"

"W-we weren't even on the Bluebloods' siiiiiide!"

When Neuro gave his reply...

"Hmm? 'Why'?"

...his smile curled into a sneer.

"Because I can, mostly. I figured, the more people for the spell, the better. Ha. And to be frank, your lives mean so little to me one way or the other."

$*$ $*$ $*$

"~~~~~~~~~~~~~~~~?!?!?!"

Everything for the nobles went red. Then they burst. Their bodies ruptured. Their minds exploded. Everything fell apart.

Only bloodstained chunks of obsidian remained—the result of those who couldn't withstand the evolution. Large masses of Father's cells. The transformation had amplified the victims' life energy, and the stones were brimming with powerful mana.

"They wouldn't pick a fight with me if they didn't think they could win. I bet Yggdra fed them a story about me being weaker because I was reborn and lost my original body. I suppose she's not *technically* wrong... But there's really no need for me to use Philosopher's Stones on *myself.*"

Neuro turned his thoughts to his foes on that distant battlefield, and he laughed at their shallow imaginations.

He had plenty of mana crystallized here, and if he combined that with the energy he'd been storing for the gate to expel his opponents from this world, he could emulate the power he'd enjoyed in his prime.

"Bear witness to Leviathan's roar."

Neuro raised his staff, and the crystals shattered. A bloodlike liquid came spraying out of them, sinking into a magic circle on the plaza grounds and dyeing its white pattern red.

Neuro chanted an incantation.

With each verse, the red light grew stronger...

...until an opening formed.

Transportation magic was Neuro's specialty. It's what had carried him from his home world to this one, and with that power he'd formed a portal between the plaza and the bottom of the ocean—

©Sacraneco

*   *   *

"Tidal Breath."

—unleashing an impossible, unthinkable amount of water.

Such was the power of Neuro's war magic.

The massive oceanic pressure forced the water straight up, transforming it into a waterfall that stretched to the heavens. Gravity's pull was no match for it, and though the friction in the air wore it down, creating a misty spray in every direction, the pillar climbed higher still.

Eventually, after shooting past mountains, punching through clouds, and escaping the atmosphere...

...it pierced clean through the planet's newest star, Ringo's military satellite.

"AHHHHHHH!"

"Ringo?! What's wrong?!"

Out of the blue, Tsukasa's fellow helicopter passenger, Ringo, let out a pained scream. When Tsukasa turned to see what was amiss, he found her grimacing.

"I-I'm...fine...," Ringo assured, removing the headset she'd been wearing over one ear. "But...it's bad. It looks like...the satellite...is down!"

"_____!"

Then...

"Tsuclawsa! There's something pawsitioned up in the sky, to the west!"

Before Tsukasa had time to think, Bearabbit reported another anomaly.

A thin structure stretched past the mountains into the sky. It resembled a piece of string from this distance.

"What is that?"

"I-it's...a furociously large column of water! It's bruin up from Freyjagard's Emperor domain, and it's so big that it reaches all the way into outer... Wh-WHAT?!"

"Bearabbit, talk to me!"

"Th-th-things are about to get grizzly! The column is falling our way! I-it's going to land right on the battlefield!!"

"_____!"

Tsukasa stared at the tower of water in disbelief. Sure enough, the threadlike pillar stretching into the sky was gradually widening, drawing nearer. A liquid blade was about to come crashing down.

CHAPTER 3

⚜ The Sarutobi Ninja Scrolls ⚜

""""Whooooa!""""

Winter was around the corner, and the new-moon night was really getting chilly. However, the air inside the traveling performers' tent in a park in Drachen's commoners' district was practically sizzling with excitement.

"Damn, how long's this troupe had that cutie?"

"What kind of diet does she use to keep her skin so smooth?"

"She's got a great rack, but her body's all sorts of toned, too. I-I'm into it!"

Drachen's commoner laborers were cheering. Work had finished for the day, so they were treating themselves to an acrobatics show while guzzling beer. Drachen was a major hub for the performing arts, so shows like this one were common. The crowd was unusually excited today, however.

The reason for their fervor stood at the center of the tent.

The spectators' eyes were bloodshot from how intently they stared. The alluring girl twirling her body in front of the tent's support post was just that beautiful. Although she was on the shorter side, she was plump in all the right places, and the contrast between her peach-blond hair and her tanned skin only made her more radiant.

Her outfit was adorned with jewels and had only barely enough fabric to count as clothing. If she shifted even slightly, you could see under her skirt. It was designed precisely with that in mind, actually. Clad in the lascivious outfit, the performer bounced her disproportionately large breasts in time with the music, then turned her crotch toward the audience and suggestively opened her legs wide and swayed her hips.

Her risqué dance hit the male laborers right in the libido, and they got fired up like never before. The crowd grew so large that it couldn't be contained in the tent.

The girl proved so attractive and deft at captivating the audience that she had to be the troupe's main dancer...

...but she wasn't.

She wasn't part of the troupe at all.

Although the girl's skin was bronzed a shade darker, she was undoubtedly Shinobu Sarutobi, prodigy journalist.

"Hey, she just winked at me!"

"What're you on about, dumbass?! She was *obviously* winking at *me*!"

"You wanna go, big guy?!"

Obviously, Shinobu hadn't come just to pole dance. She was here to retrieve a wayward teammate, Masato Sanada, and his apprentice, Roo. That was easier said than done, as Freyjagard was trying to forestall any move the Prodigies might make. Helping free Yamato had made Neuro an outright enemy, and war had already begun.

Security checkpoints leading to Drachen, the enemy capital, were strict. Shinobu was skilled enough to find a way around them, but their sheer number would have made that a huge amount of work. It also would've required a lot of time, and detours always carried their own risks. Ultimately, Shinobu elected to brazenly stroll through the checkpoints.

She'd joined with a caravan that already had permission to enter Drachen and blended in as one of its members. Facial recognition software was centuries away on this world, and the troupe's members weren't going to expose Shinobu and risk delaying their own journey.

Shinobu's plan worked like a charm. She moved deep into enemy territory—all the way to the commoners' district on the outer edge of Drachen, no less—and all without a fight.

Masato was in Drachen's imperial castle.

His phone was turned off, but Ringo had modded the Prodigies' mobile devices to ping her satellite with their current locations every so often as long as they had a charge, so at least Shinobu knew where he was.

The only obstacles were the two fortress walls separating the commoners' district, the nobles' district, and the castle. Both of the structures were impressively tall, but Shinobu could scale a building with only the tiniest handholds. Even rust was enough for her to grip. She'd be over the walls in no time.

However, it was too early in the evening. Commoners were still awake drinking. There were too many watchful eyes for her to try anything. She'd have to wait until the city was asleep.

Until then…

…I gotta make sure I really get things popping in here—to make it up to the girl I replaced, *if nothing else.*

""""What…?!""""

Not a moment later, a different kind of stir ran through the hyped-up audience. The people looked aghast.

Shinobu had been moving to show off her body's curves, but

now her movements were quicker. She shifted from pole dancing to raw feats of athleticism.

"Damn, how's she moving like that?!"

"That upper-body strength is nuts!"

"I can't believe what I'm seeing..."

With one hand clamped on the tent's support pole, Shinobu took a stroll in midair as casually as she might walk on the ground. Then she coiled her legs around the pole and twirled at an incredible pace. To top it all off, she held her whole body out like a flag.

On Earth, pole dancing was strongly associated with strip shows, but it originated from a wrestling-based form of gymnastics called Mallakhamba. The grueling exercise explored the limits of the human body using a single pole. It required immense strength, even from a ninja. Sweat beaded on Shinobu's beautifully outstretched legs and proudly displayed breasts. The droplets glistened in the light of the tent's bonfires.

However...

"""" """"
....

...none cheered as they had previously.

The men still watched Shinobu, but the lust had faded from their eyes. They waited with bated breath for her to finish the performance.

Rather than fervor and enthusiasm, there was tense silence, which persisted until Shinobu spun her way down from the very top of the pole. She concluded her show by landing soundlessly upon the ground with her legs in a perfect 180-degree split.

""""WHOOOOOOOOOOOOOOO!!!!""""

The audience offered an earsplitting round of applause.

"That was INCREDIBLE! You're somethin' else, Shino!"

"That last part! *Whew!* I couldn't tear my eyes away!"

"I watched so hard, I accidentally sobered up! I'll take another round!"

Erotic dancing existed as a way for apprentice acrobats to get crowds excited despite lacking the perfected skills of a master. Seeing a show begin that way and then become something much more was a huge surprise. Shinobu's performance earned the most excitement of any that night. The crowd cheered even harder when she waved and smiled. The booze practically sold itself.

Shinobu's work for the troupe she'd infiltrated ended as a rousing success.

"All right, everyone, that's a wrap!"

""""Cheers!""""

Once the audience cleared out of the park, the troupe members celebrated the show's completion. Shinobu took part as well, of course. She emptied her wooden tankard of ale in a single swig...

"Whew! That hits the spot after a hard day's work!"

"I gotta say, Shino, you really saved our butts today."

"No kiddin'. When our dancer went missing out of nowhere, we had no idea what we were gonna do tonight. Who'd've thought a bona fide virtuoso like you would show up and agree to fill in? I guess we've still got a bit of luck left."

...and the troupe leader and his wife thanked her from their seats beside her.

Shinobu was behind the apprentice dancer's disappearance, but the couple had no way of knowing that. It was only natural for them to be so grateful to the disguised Shinobu, who'd approached the troupe claiming she wished to join the world of performing arts.

The journalist ninja smiled without the tiniest bit of guilt. "Ha-ha-ha. Please, I'm no virtuoso. Just a girl from the countryside with big dreams of being a dancer."

"Nah, Shino, you're something else. That pole dancing of yours was in a league all its own."

"Those geezers were giving you some of the *sleaziest* looks I've ever seen, but for those last bits, they were so captured by your performance that sex was the furthest thing from their minds."

"Hey, lemme check out your arm for a sec. I wanna see how ripped someone has to get to hold their whole body up the way you did."

"Whaaat? C'mon, I'm no muscle head."

"Yeah, yeah, we'll see about— Wait, it's so thin!"

"No way. How did you swing around so freely when your limbs are that dainty?"

"See, the trick there is you gotta kind of use your whoole body," Shinobu explained.

Before she knew it, the entire troupe was gathered around her. It was the first time any of them saw a trick like that, and they peppered her with questions about how much she worked out and gawked in astonishment at her slender arms.

If anything, Shinobu's arms were skinnier than those of the average girl on the street. However, just beneath the skin was a layer of the most pliable muscle around. The Sarutobis had been a ninja clan for generations, and they'd developed a training regime that focused on muscle quality instead of mass. Beauty was an important weapon in the *kunoichi* arsenal, so it had to be preserved. Shinobu had used that training to its utmost and cultivated a body that, much like a leopard's, appeared lithe at first glance but was rich with unseen power. It was the perfect ninja build.

On top of that, Shinobu's martial arts enabled her to augment her physical abilities in all sorts of other ways. She could support her body with her bones instead of her muscles or use centrifugal force to counteract some of her weight. With all those factors combined, an unrehearsed dance was child's play.

None of it would've been possible if she wasn't a genius hailed the world over as a prodigy, though. Understanding Shinobu's techniques was one thing, but replicating them was impossible.

The troupe leader must have realized that, for he donned his business face. "Shino, what do you say to becoming a permanent member?"

He couldn't let talent like hers get away. The offer was the rational choice for a troupe leader, and all his members voiced their approval.

"Good call, boss! C'mon, Shino, we'd love to have you!"

"With you as our main dancer, the sky would be the limit. We might even get shows in the nobles' district! At least think it over, okay?"

However, Shinobu gave them an apologetic reply…

"Oh man, that's so kind of you to offer. But I can't. I want to see if I can join Luvirche and really put my skills to the test."

…and fed them the same lie she'd used to join with the group in the first place.

The troupe members all slumped.

"Yeah, that figures."

"If Luvirche's on the table…then I guess we can't stop you."

Luvirche was one of the biggest performing companies in the empire. Its theatrical focus differed a bit from this troupe's acrobatics. Still, Luvirche's plays tended to incorporate flashy, intense action scenes, so they certainly had need of nimble employees. There was no point in trying to talk "Shino" out of auditioning with one of the industry leaders. A two-bit show that earned its keep shilling drinks to manual laborers couldn't compete.

Still…

"A-are you sure about this? Luvirche is the big leagues, yeah, but their test is no joke. Plus, even if you get in, it'll be ages before you're big enough to make it on their billboards. Why put yourself through all that hardship when you could just stay with us and have a good time?"

…the performers hated to see Shinobu go.

Considering how young and attractive Shinobu was, some of the troupe members might have developed feelings for her. Whatever the reason, they didn't want her to leave.

However…

"Leave the girl be, Ted."

…the troupe leader's wife told off the member who'd spoken up.

"With talent and skill like Shino's, she'll be up on them big Luvirche posters before you know it."

The troupe leader nodded. "Missing out on one so able sucks, but if she's made up her mind, then she's made up her mind. I'll be rooting for you, Shino. Break a leg on that Luvirche application test."

Shinobu smiled. "Thanks, boss! That means so much!"

Shinobu felt pangs of guilt for all the lies, but she was a consummate ninja and didn't let it show on her face.

"But if you don't make it into Luvirche, you'll always have a place here with us," the troupe leader added.

"Ha-ha. If I fail, I think I might take you up on that."

After the attempts to recruit Shinobu died down, one of the

middle-aged performers started twirling his mustache with a grim expression. "Luvirche, huh... For bein' the best troupe in the empire, feels like I haven't heard much good about them lately."

The troupe leader and his wife nodded sagely. "Ah, right. That thing about them going up to Elm and putting on a show criticizing Emperor Lindworm."

Shinobu heard about that back when she visited Elm. One of the Reform Party candidates, Glaux, had put together a dastardly scheme, and part of it involved Luvirche drumming up favor for the armed attack on the emperor that the Reform Party sought at the time.

"People are even saying that the Bluebloods put Lurviche up to it."

"The Bluebloods got stamped out in the civil war. I wouldn't be surprised if Emperor Lindworm and the Four Grandmasters put down Luvirche for supporting them."

Luvirche had definitely picked the wrong side in that conflict, and the company could find itself ostracized from the nobles' district for it. The troupe began talking shop, noting they'd have to be careful who they supported in the future, too.

However...

"This is ridiculous."

...a young stagehand drinking on a wooden crate was having none of it.

"You really think that the War Emperor is petty enough to care about little stuff like that?"

"What do you mean, Flit?"

"Emperor Lindworm is far more broad-minded than any of you give him credit for. No other ruler can surpass him."

Something about Flit the stagehand's statement caught Shinobu's attention. It wasn't her ninja instincts at work but the intuition she'd honed as a journalist. There was something more than blind faith behind his words. Where did it stem from?

Shinobu was never one to let a hunch go unexplored. "Wow, Flit. You think really highly of Emperor Lindworm, huh?"

"Of course I do. What sort of good imperial citizen *doesn't* believe in their emperor?"

"Is that all there is to it, though? I dunno, it just sounded like you had some specific reason for your faith..."

The question was pretty intrusive, so Shinobu softened it with an adorable tilt of the head. A cute girl could loosen guys' lips easily, and Flit was no exception.

"Well, *both of them are dead now*, so I guess it's probably fine to talk about," he said. "I saw something back during the Yamato War. Something that showed me just how great he is."

"Oh yeah, that's right. You served in those days," the troupe leader's wife remarked.

All eyes were on Flit. "What was it? What'd you see?" someone asked.

Flit seemed to enjoy the attention, and he ostentatiously cleared his throat. "There was a coup staged during the Yamato War, you see, and a savage attempt was made on Emperor Lindworm's life. It failed, though, so I guess I should call it an attempted coup, but still.

"The whole thing was put under a gag order, which is why no one heard about it. But I was there. It was on a moonless night, like this one, and the attack was orchestrated by Granzham von Blumheart.

"He had a coconspirator, and if you can believe it, it was a man who was later granted a dukedom and became one of His Grace's most loyal retainers—Oslo el Gustav."

"_____?!"

Not even Shinobu could hide her surprise. That was the last name she'd expected to hear.

Flit watched her reaction with great amusement.

By his account, the Lindworm dynasty started a war three years ago to demolish the neighboring country of Yamato and to seize control over the entire continent. The Freyjagard ambassador's covert operation succeeded better than all expectations, and after dealing a crippling blow to the Yamato empire, the imperial army pushed into enemy territory, crushing the routed samurai as they went. After a month, Freyjagard nearly secured victory. There was a handful of warriors still fighting using guerrilla tactics, but everyone knew it was only a matter of time until they fell.

But that confidence made the imperials complacent, lax. All of them, from the knights, to the mages, to the lowliest grunts, let their guards down. And on the day in question, when Flit was protecting Lindworm as he slept, he got sloppy, too.

That's when the coup happened.

The emperor's guard was thinnest after he retired for the night, and Blumheart and Gustav—just the two of them—decided to spring their surprise attack then.

For a coup, the plan was pretty simple. As Lindworm stood at the tent's entrance on his way to bed, Gustav would approach from behind and hurl Rage Soleil at him. Gustav was already the Imperial Prime Mage by this point, and the attack hinged on his outstanding combat capabilities. The coup required only two people, and no one else knew of the scheme.

Flit, who stood next to the tent's entrance, braced himself for death when he realized what was happening.

However...

* * *

"He parried Rage Soleil with a *sword*...?!"

Flit nodded as Shinobu gaped in disbelief.

"That's right. He took Gustav's trump card, the war magic spell Rage Soleil that had burned a Yamato base to the ground in a single night, and shattered it to pieces with a swing of his massive blade."

Lindworm's golden sword was as long as he was tall, and when the Rage Soleil bore down on him, he *pulverized* it effortlessly.

Blumheart and Gustav had believed the plan already succeeded and were so astonished to discover the true outcome that they forgot to run. Nearby soldiers surrounded them in moments.

It took a few men apiece to pin the pair of insurgents to the ground, but once they were subdued, Lindworm posed them a question. He wished to know why they'd turned against their master, a man they ought to revere. What had driven them to action?

By that point, the two failed assailants had already accepted their fates. Their failure was absolute, and they saw no point in trying to resist. They told the emperor they'd done it for the powerless masses, to create a world where everyone could live in peace without fear of oppression.

They told Lindworm about how hordes of people were suffering under his militaristic rule. Plenty of blood had been shed between the civil war against the old administration and the empire's invasions and annexations of its smaller neighbors to the south and the west. Blumheart and Gustav demanded to know when Lindworm would be sated. The casualties continued to pile up as Freyjagard advanced into Yamato, a nation with nothing to offer the empire.

Lindworm was a lion running roughshod over the entire world, and as Blumheart and Gustav saw it, they had a duty to stop him.

Flit and the other soldiers got ready to run the two rebels through. Freyjagardian society operated on survival of the fittest, and this pair had gone against the strongest man in the empire. Extenuating circumstances or not, it was a crime deserving of execution.

However...

...Lindworm spoke.

He faced those who'd threatened his life and said, "Release them."

Lindworm's inexplicable order sent a stir through the troops. Still, they weren't about to disobey a command from the emperor. They immediately released the two captives and sheathed their swords.

Blumheart and Gustav couldn't make sense of Lindworm's actions, regarding the man with bewilderment.

"Y-Your Grace?"

"...What's the meaning of this, Emperor Lindworm?"

Lindworm responded with a question. "Blumheart. Gustav. You spoke of cutting me down for the sake of the people, but what then? Would you two take the throne yourselves? Do you believe that would create a world free of suffering?"

"Gustav and I would put in the necessary work to—"

"It would fail."

Lindworm silenced Blumheart.

"Slaying me and ending the war with Yamato won't stop all conflict. So long as impostors lacking the necessary qualities pretend to be kings and members of the rabble with no capacity to rule act as nobles holding dominion over others, there will be bloodshed. Jealousy and greed will drive them to it. You two will only become another pair of links in that chain. If you truly care for the populace and wish for a world where none need suffer, then know this:

"What this world needs is a flawless ruler. One who will not be beaten. One who will not perish. One who will not err.

"A world of hegemony, ruled by Lindworm von Freyjagard and Lindworm von Freyjagard alone."

"«« ....!»»"

Lindworm's declaration struck Blumheart and Gustav speechless.

"Your Grace, you believe that none can defeat you?"

"I do. Not you, or the nobles, or the rulers of any foreign states."

"And you…you trust that no matter how much time passes, you won't die?"

"I do. Peace that only lasts a generation is but a trifle. I shall reign over this world as its ruler in perpetuity."

"A-and…you believe…that your decisions are always correct?"

"I do. You need only follow me with faith."

"This is DERANGED!" Blumheart had finally managed to squeeze questions from his pale, trembling lips, and upon hearing Lindworm's fantastical delusions, he turned furious. "I was right— you need to be stopped! All the blood you've shed, the bodies you've left in your wake, it was for…this lunacy?! You, a single man, seek to rule the world forever? That's impossible!"

If Freyjagard bought into this madness, the empire would fall. Blumheart drew the saber hanging from his waist and leveled it at Lindworm.

*　　*　　*

"In all my days, have I ever spoken a single falsehood?"

"I..."
"..."

Lindworm focused his gaze upon Blumheart and Gustav, and the look in his eyes was so enthralling, they forgot to breathe.

There was no false bravado to be found in him.

Lindworm wasn't bluffing. He spoke with true conviction—the belief of a man who knew where he was going, who trusted his legs to get him there. In his eyes, his goal was attainable.

"You may not believe me now, but once this war awakens *the true power within me*, my capabilities will be plain to all. Everyone will see who this world truly belongs to, and when that time comes, I will abolish the imperial aristocracy and take on the totality of the burdens too great for my subjects to bear."

Blumheart didn't have the faintest clue what to make of that. However, Gustav fell to his knees as though struck by lightning.

Lindworm strode calmly between the two...

"In all of creation, I am the sole being fit to rule from on high. Put your faith in me and in me alone."

...and left them behind.

"...It was crazy talk. We all knew that Emperor Lindworm was strong. Hell, he might even be powerful enough to unite the whole world. But still... Getting rid of the foreign rulers is one thing, but there's no way he could govern the world if he abolished the aristocracy on top of that."

It simply wasn't realistic.

Blumheart and Gustav had known that, as did everyone else present for the speech. Flit recalled how he and the rest of the soldiers had agreed with the two failed assassins.

"But at the same time...there was something about him that made you believe he could do it."

It should have been easy to write Lindworm off as a babbling fool, yet no one present had managed to denounce him.

That unwavering confidence brooked no argument. It was as though Lindworm knew he was *more than human*. If he truly was a flawless ruler who would never fail or die...

"...Then I want to live under his rule. Don't get me wrong—Duke Gustav took things too far. But his belief in Emperor Lindworm was justified.

"Those Republic of Elm fools ramble about freedom and independence and commoners becoming emperors, but will that really make them happy? The emperor's right. There aren't that many people worthy of governing others.

"All that stuff about how making commoners into rulers will lead to a government that's kind to all...*that's just as much bullshit as Freyjagard.*

"When someone gets power, they cling to it. They grow suspicious of others and suppress enemies to solidify their strength. It's in our nature. The only difference is the people can't complain because they asked for freedom. Empire or Elm, if both are gonna feed me the same crap, I'd at least like to live under an absolute ruler I can trust."

"........."

Shinobu voiced no agreement or opposition.

She had nothing to say. Flit was describing the ultimate fate of democracy, something her world had witnessed many times already.

It was late into the night, and all the sounds of the city were gone, save the occasional dog bark.

Once they finished their party, the troupe members dispersed to the respective tavern rooms they'd booked. The troupe was kind enough to get Shinobu a room, too, and she headed there. Upon arriving, she spread out her ninja tools on the bed to confirm everything was in order for her infiltration mission.

As she inspected her gear...

"Lindworm von Freyjagard, huh?"

...she thought back to Flit's story.

Lindworm had referred to his *"true power."* From the sound of it, Neuro and the other grandmasters probably fed him a couple of half-truths to embolden him while leaving out anything that would interfere with their plan.

In a sense, Lindworm was one of the grandmasters' victims, too. Talking things out with him and winning him over like Tsukasa had suggested was still a possible option.

But on the other hand...

...Shinobu got the feeling that exposing the grandmasters' scheme wouldn't change Lindworm's mind. From his perspective, Neuro and the others were day-one allies, whereas the Prodigies were a group whittling away at the empire's territory and obstructing its goal of world domination. There was no question which side

Lindworm would trust, and the Prodigies wouldn't be able to prove anything until it was too late.

"If he really destroyed Rage Soleil that easily...then there's gotta be something pretty funky about Lindworm himself."

Not even Ringo's antiair missiles could bring down Rage Soleil, yet Lindworm had smashed the spell to bits in a single motion. Whatever his deal, he was no pushover. Yggdra had told Shinobu and the others that Father required a suitable vessel and that the grandmasters waited for such an exceptional person. The grandmasters were undoubtedly a threat, but Lindworm deserved great caution, too.

"An absolute ruler..."

Never beaten. Never perishing. Never erring.

A world controlled by an unquestionable leader meant everyone except that leader would be equal. It would create a perfect world without war.

According to Flit's story, Lindworm sought the ultimate form of monarchy.

"He almost reminds me of Tsukes."

Tsukasa Mikogami and Lindworm both had their sights fixed on the same goal: a world of equality that was free of war, where people could live in peace. The only difference was the route. Tsukasa knew that people were born with evil in them, but he chose to believe in their inherent goodness, and he sought a society of people supporting one another. Lindworm believed in none but himself and desired to rule as a supreme overlord.

One chose faith; the other chose fetters.

The two were as different as could be...and yet...

If—if—War Emperor Lindworm was genuinely unbeatable, undying, and unerring, if he was a prodigy politician in every sense, then how would Tsukasa feel about opposing him?

When the young prime minister thought of those he'd let *slip through his fingers on his quest to save as many as possible*, how would he—?

"!"

Shinobu's mind was straying to a dark place, and she clapped herself on the cheeks. She didn't need to indulge those ideas. At the moment, she had more urgent matters.

"I've got a job to do."

She had to find Masato and Roo, then tell them about Neuro's plan.

Shinobu had known Masato forever and understood that for all his wits and pragmatism, he wasn't the sort to let a friend die to further his ends. He saved that for enemies and those he acknowledged as rivals. Once Masato learned what Neuro was after, he'd come back, and the Prodigies would be at full strength again.

That needed to happen. Shinobu couldn't afford any screwups. She focused and strapped on her ninja tools.

Once ready, she opened the large wooden box in the corner of the room.

"Mmmph......!"

Inside was a girl two or three years Shinobu's junior. Her hands and feet were bound, and her mouth was gagged. Fear shone in the girl's teary eyes, but Shinobu seemed unaffected, hoisting the captive up and laying her on the bed.

Then...

"Sorry. I know it must've been scary."

...she offered an apology.

The girl was the troupe's usual dancer. She hadn't gone missing—Shinobu had kidnapped her.

"The nice innkeeper'll come to the room for the wake-up call tomorrow morning. You can have her untie you."

Shinobu placed a letter of apology addressed to the troupe beside the girl, then pushed the wooden window open.

The night beyond the tavern room was pitch-black. This world lacked electricity, so evenings were unfathomably dark, even more so tonight because of the new moon.

There was no better time to run a covert operation.

"All righty... Let's do this."

Shinobu leaped into the dark.

No roadside braziers lit her way. All Shinobu had to guide her was the faint glow from the stars. However, that meager light was enough for her honed ninja eyes. Commoners' district roofs became stepping stones as she hopped silently across the city.

Eventually, she arrived at a wall seventy feet high—her first obstacle. This was the barrier separating the commoners' district from the nobles' one. Drachen's three sections were separated by two immense, defensive bulwarks. Freyjagard was one of the greatest military powers in the world, and its heavily fortified capital stood as a testament to that fact.

Breaching the wall was impossible for most. However, prodigy journalist Shinobu Sarutobi was a different sort. This master of intelligence could infiltrate Air Force One if she so desired. She hooked her fingers into the seams between the wall stones, then climbed the vertical face as swiftly as she would a ladder. In no time at all, she was up and over, crossing the divide between commoners and nobles.

Shinobu dropped seventy feet and landed without a sound. It was a prodigious feat if ever there was one.

She had moved undetected. No one was aware of her presence. However...

*   *   *

"!!!!"

...the moment she touched the ground, a terrible chill ran through her.

Shinobu gasped.

"..."

Meanwhile, a middle-aged man stood quickly from his seat at the bar in a guardroom within the fortress between the commoners' and nobles' districts. He was tall, lean, and blessed with an impressive beard. Unlike the rest of the soldiers, he wore a well-tailored butler uniform.

"Hmm? What's up, Mr. Ninja?"

"You gotta hit the can or something? Damn, I woulda thought Yamato ninjas could hold their beer better. That's weak, man!"

"C'mon, drink up! If you don't take this mug, how am I supposed to know you're one of us?!"

The uniform-clad man shook his head. "I wish I could accept your offer, believe me. But I fear I cannot."

"Hmm?"

"It would seem that a crafty little rat has snuck its way inside. Pardon me." By the time he excused himself, the uniformed man had vanished.

"Huh?"

"What?!"

"Where'd he go?"

It was like he'd never been there at all.

Cold sweat ran from Shinobu's pores as she raced through the nobles' district. She didn't bother to keep silent anymore, instead running as fast as she could.

Shit, shit, shit, shit, shit…!

Someone had noticed Shinobu, despite her flawless technique. She'd entered the nobles' district silently and unseen, without leaving the slightest indication of her presence.

And yet someone had detected her. They'd picked up on the *minuscule discomfort they'd felt when Shinobu cleared the wall.*

No matter how expertly someone disguised their movements, it wouldn't work on an opponent capable of doing the same. The more perfect the stealth, the *easier* for an ace opponent to recognize it.

In short, Shinobu's foe was a ninja. One with skills on par with hers—perhaps better.

"…"

Shinobu had an inkling of who it might be.

During her time gathering information about this world, she'd heard about a rogue ninja from Yamato who had survived in the societal underworld on nothing but his own strength. He was an assassin who worked for anyone with coin.

Shinobu had witnessed how powerful Yamato's people were during the last war, and she knew she couldn't afford to fight one of them now. So she headed toward the castle, moving as fast as her legs would carry her…

"…"

…and realized that her enemy had circled around her and waited atop the roof of a nearby mansion.

"As a *kunoichi*, you should have known there was no escaping from Sasuke the Black Spider."

"...Yeah, that tracks."

The man before Shinobu was tall and lean, and despite the darkness and the sloped roof's poor footing, his center of balance was solid as he stood atop the building's peak.

There was no mistaking it. This man was a ninja.

Worse, the name he gave was worrying.

"I've heard a lot of stories about you. You used to be head of the Special Forces, right?"

"I fear I cannot profess to know of you... But I can tell you're no Yamato ninja. Your face is new to me."

The man stroked his beard as he fixed his eagle-sharp eyes on Shinobu. The gesture made him look off guard, but it was clearly for show. He carefully kept his limbs slack, ready to respond to anything Shinobu tried.

If she came at him unprepared, she would suffer a brutal counterattack.

And so...

"Well, sure. That's 'cause I'm not a ninja. I'm a journalist."

...she readied a *shuriken* in each hand while keeping a close eye out for any sudden moves from Sasuke.

Sasuke glared at the girl, recognizing her hostility...

"Yield now or this will hurt more than it has to."

...and demanded her surrender.

His voice was deep and level, like a nightjar's cry echoing through the dark. It rang with the sound of a man supremely confident in his abilities.

©Sacraneco

However…

"…Look, if I had more time to work with, I might just take you up on that."

…Shinobu hadn't come this far to quit.

She liked to avoid battles when possible, but there was a time to flee and a time to fight, and she was wise enough to know the difference.

"Unfortunately, I'm in a hurry. I'm coming through, whether you like it or not."

"Then you are a fool."

"Oh, we'll see about that."

Shinobu had to strike now, and so she took the initiative. Thirty feet separated her and Sasuke, and she hurled her two *shuriken* at his feet. The goal was to restrict his mobility.

However, Sasuke wasn't about to be disabled that easily. He evaded by sliding backward, then raced across the roof's perimeter so he could rush Shinobu from the side. The footing was slanted, but it didn't slow him down.

"Hah!"

This time, it was Shinobu's turn to react. She pulled out another set of *shuriken* from her holster and sent them flying at her foe to pressure him as he moved in. Ideally, that would've been enough to cause Sasuke to trip and tumble off the building.

That's asking a bit much, though. Instead…

In addition to the standard iron *shuriken* in her holster, Shinobu also carried "shadow" *shuriken* that had been specially treated to be as matte as possible. Spotting them on a moonless night was impossible even for Shinobu…

"Wh—?!"

…and yet they weren't enough.

"Metal that doesn't reflect the light? How novel."

To Shinobu's astonishment, Sasuke casually snatched every *shuriken* thrown at him right out of the air.

"Playthings will not avail you here."

"Rgh..."

Performing a feat like that should've required seeing the *shuriken*. Was Sasuke's eyesight better than Shinobu's? The girl winced in frustration but kept focused on dealing with her opponent's charge. She leaped backward and moved away as far as Sasuke ran in.

That hardly solved the problem, though.

Now that Shinobu had retreated, she had to deal with being stuck on the roof's edge. And judging by Sasuke's attacks...

"Hyah!"

...it seemed he'd been trying to push her to this point all along.

He swung his arm. Was he about to throw a projectile? That was the first thing Shinobu suspected, and she readied a pair of *kunai* to intercept. However...

...she realized that Sasuke was unarmed.

But then why—?

Suddenly, Shinobu spotted a long, thin object glinting in the faint starlight.

"!"

A series of slashes came hurtling down, deadly and invisible. Fortunately, Shinobu picked up on the slightest warning, giving her a chance to react.

She swung her *kunai* with all her might.

The friction of metal on metal sent a shower of sparks cascading through the air, and that tiny flash revealed the nature of Sasuke's attack.

He was using string—or rather, steel wire.

By taking advantage of the spirits' ability to manipulate objects on a microscopic level, one could manufacture blades as thin as a string. The technique was thought to be exclusive to Imperial Prime Mages, however. This was how the ninja known as the Black Spider killed his foes. Armed with that steel wire, he could slice his prey to ribbons, even from a distance.

Shinobu expertly parried the attacks, but...

...*I'm not gonna be able to keep this up forever.*

Sasuke's strikes were so relentless that Shinobu didn't have time to so much as blink. She could feel her limit approaching quickly.

Staying on the back foot wasn't an option.

While using both hands to defend, Shinobu found room in between clashes to hurl a flash-bang.

A blast like white lightning filled the air. It was too bright for people to see through, making it functionally similar to total darkness.

The white void obscured Shinobu from her opponent's view...

"......?!"

...yet the Black Spider continued to attack, undeterred.

"I've trained to follow my mark without sight."

Shinobu had hoped the flash-bang would provide cover for her escape, but her opponent beat her to the punch. The moment she threw it, Sasuke charged across the rooftop and closed the gap. Now he was close enough to launch a palm strike directly at her face.

"Hrah!"

"Hyah!"

Shinobu responded resolutely to Sasuke's challenge, and the two began a close-quarters duel so fierce, they didn't have time to breathe.

Sasuke appeared to have bracers and chain mail hidden

beneath his clothes, as whenever Shinobu went in with her *kunai*, her attacks bounced right off. *Kunai* weren't designed for slashing, and Shinobu doubted they'd break through Sasuke's defenses. Cutting the armor wasn't an option.

However, Shinobu could put all her strength into a thrust. That might do the trick. The *kunoichi* continued fighting, searching for an opportunity...

Now!

...then wove through Sasuke's tempest of strikes to stab him in the side.

Unfortunately, Sasuke had left that opening on purpose.

Shinobu's thrust found only empty air, and Sasuke snagged her outstretched arm with his own. Shinobu's fist was still clenched tight around her *kunai*, and Sasuke caught the hand in his armpit, then pressed up on her elbow with the back of his hand.

A horrible creaking accompanied the hot pain that shot through Shinobu.

This is bad...

Sasuke was going to break her arm.

Upon realizing that, Shinobu acted fast and leaped hard into the air. By taking the strength her opponent was using to snap her arm and turn it against him, she managed to jump over his head, break free from his hold...

"Hiyah!"

...and launch a kick at the base of his skull.

Shinobu put her full weight into the attack. This was no time for mercy. She felt her attack connect, but the impact left her speechless.

Wha...?

It felt like she'd kicked a mighty tree with deep roots. Sasuke's center of balance was so low, it was hard to believe he stood on something as uneven as a roof.

The man didn't so much as twitch. Shinobu's hopes of concussing him were dashed.

Sasuke fixed his gaze on her as she fled into the air. His eyes were like an insect's, cold and unfeeling, and at that moment, a realization dawned on Shinobu.

This fight was kill or be killed. She was going to have to do whatever it took.

"Hiyah!"

As Shinobu passed over her foe's head, she threw two *kunai* toward where she'd been a moment earlier. Naturally, Sasuke wasn't amateur enough to be hit by such an obvious counterattack. He looked back over his shoulder and casually swatted the *kunai* away.

That came as no surprise to Shinobu. His swatting the two *kunai* away was a foregone conclusion. And knowing that he'd block them, Shinobu had added another attack into the mix.

She used her tongue to fish out the deadly weapon she kept hidden behind her molars...

"Ptoo!"

...then pursed her lips and spat it out.

Sasuke's hands were both occupied by the *kunai*, so he had no way of reacting. Shinobu's weapon sank into his thigh. The object in question was a thin needle, one coated in...

"Fugu, hmm?"

"GAH???"

The next thing Shinobu knew, Sasuke's fist slammed into her abdomen. She felt the shock travel through her abs to her back, shattering ribs as it moved.

Her body went flying across the roof, and although she

managed to stick the landing, her expression was pale with grim shock. She'd hit Sasuke with a poison needle. The toxin was a special Sarutobi compound derived from fugu. It was deadly enough to kill big game instantly.

And yet...

"I've been ingesting it since I was eight to build up a tolerance."

...it didn't slow Sasuke in the slightest.

He casually plucked the needle from his thigh and flicked it away.

"Rrr...rrr...gh...!"

Shinobu groaned in agony at her fractured ribs as she bemoaned her miscalculation. There was no such thing as tetrodotoxin immunity. A person couldn't build up immunity. Scientifically speaking, it was impossible. However, it was clearly the case with Sasuke.

I bet I have those experiments Yggdra talked about to thank for it.

A thousand years ago, the Yamato people's ancestors were subjected to forced evolution, and the results were still evident in the nation's modern citizens, most notably in their preeminent physical abilities.

The fact was, their bodies were different from most others'. Shinobu couldn't afford to base her assumptions on how normal people functioned in this fight. She should have accounted for outliers.

"Pant, pant...!"

Things are going south fast. This guy...is on par with Shishi.

Sasuke's raw combat abilities were probably a little lower than Shishi's, but the difference was negligible. Either way, Shinobu was no contest.

Only Aoi could beat such opponents in a straight fight.

After her brutal thrashing, Shinobu conceded that her chances of victory were slim and growing worse by the moment. Cold sweat formed on her forehead from the stress and pain. She racked her brain for an idea…

"Hey! What the hell do you think you're doing up there?!"

…but, as though to salt the wound, the situation worsened.

Nobles' district soldiers were gathering after hearing the commotion.

"Isn't that the ninja Marquis Northheim hired?!"

"That's Master Heidekker's mansion, you barbarians! Get down from there at once!"

Guards surrounded the mansion Shinobu and Sasuke were fighting on. There was nowhere for the prodigy journalist to run. She bit her lip, at a total loss for what to do…

Wait a minute…

…when she got an idea.

Shinobu would be done for if the imperial soldiers used their superior numbers to cut off all avenues of escape, so why didn't Sasuke have the guards do as much from the start? He'd cut her off, suggesting he knew her route. Relaying orders to soldiers should have been well within his capabilities. He didn't need to go out of his way to take Shinobu on alone.

But he did…

That's it!

Shinobu's flash of insight came not from her ninja skills but from the intuition she'd honed collecting information about and observing people as a journalist. And because of that, Shinobu was confident she was right.

The girl leaped from the roof with aplomb, casting herself into the sea of torches carried by the assembled guards.

"Tch!"

Sasuke's expression was placid as a mask this whole time, but now he grimaced slightly. He hurled a *kunai* to pick Shinobu out of the air.

The High School Prodigy had expected this, however. She unwound the scarf around her neck and swatted the projectile away. Just like Tsukasa's jacket, her scarf was custom-made and designed to be stab-resistant and bulletproof. No *kunai* would ever pierce it.

The moment Shinobu landed...

"Agh! She actually jumped!"

"Catch her! Don't let that girl get away!"

"Wh-who is this chick?! She's so fast!"

...she charged into the soldiers' ranks and wove around them, causing a huge commotion.

All the while, Sasuke did nothing.

He could have used his steel wire to slice her and the soldiers to bits, but he didn't. That required an authority he lacked. The nobles' district was home to those aristocrats who ran the Freyjagard government, and their private forces defended it. The thing was, those hired soldiers were *assets*. Damaging someone else's assets could spark infighting among the nobility.

For all his skill, Sasuke was only a vagrant mercenary. He didn't have the permission to instigate a conflict without his patron's approval, so he couldn't get another aristocrat's guards caught up in his attacks.

Shinobu's assessment was right on the mark...

"Dammit, where is she?! Where'd she go?!"

"Find her! FIND HER!"

...and the qualities that made her who she was allowed her to give her veteran ninja opponent the slip.

While Shinobu escaped...

"You struggle in vain."

...Sasuke let out an exasperated sigh.

Shinobu and Sasuke's battle ended indecisively, thanks to interference from an outside group of private soldiers. Sasuke had informed the rest of Marquis Northheim's troops about the intruder before disappearing from the guard station earlier, and a short while after the fight, his colleagues arrived on the scene.

"SASUKE! Where is that bastard?!" Forstner, the middle-aged Gold Knight who managed Northheim's men, was furious. Anger and drink colored his face bright red. "Where is he, dammit?! I swear, when I get my hands on him...!"

"Wait, huh? I could've sworn he was just here..."

"That sonofabitch, running off without my leave..."

Forstner's fists shook. It was hard to blame him for being mad. His job was to supervise Northheim's soldiers, and while Sasuke's admission into the ranks had been abrupt, he was one of them now. Any blame for his misconduct would fall on Forstner.

This incident was no exception.

"Well, well, well. This is a problem, now, isn't it? I really must request that you keep your subordinates on a tighter leash."

"...Well, if it isn't Heidekker's lapdog."

Heidekker's soldiers had been shouting at Shinobu and Sasuke during their battle, and their leader, Gold Knight Dante, chastised Forstner with a look of open annoyance decorating his handsome face.

Dante was Forstner's junior by more than a decade, and while they both held the rank of Gold Knight, Forstner saw Dante as an immature greenhorn. Being on the receiving end of his disappointment was the height of humiliation. However, the sad truth was that Heidekker's land fell under Dante's jurisdiction, and it had been Forstner's responsibility to stop Sasuke from getting into a fight and damaging Heidekker's roof. It pained Forstner to do so, but he had no choice but to bow his head low.

"I apologize for the trouble our numbskull caused."

"Look, as an imperial knight, I have no qualms about assisting you in putting down those who would harm our empire... However, I must insist that you cover the repair bill."

"Of course. I take full responsibility, and I'll personally inform Marquis Northheim about the—"

"Sir Dante!" A soldier came rushing over and interrupted the Gold Knights' conversation. He was one of Dante's subordinates who'd been combing to find Shinobu.

"You have news?" Dante asked, and the soldier straightened up.

"When we searched the neighborhood, we discovered that someone opened an entrance to the old tunnels! We suspect the intruder used it to slip underground!"

"The old tunnels," Dante mused. "Ah yes, I remember now."

"What are you on about?"

"Dear me, Forstner. And you call yourself a member of the capital guard? It would be best if you hit the books, my friend. Long ago, back when Drachen had but the one exterior fortress wall, the city guard used the old tunnels as emergency passageways."

In the early days, the underground passages stretched beneath all of Drachen, covering everything from the castle to the commoners' district. However, with the introduction of the new city defense system thirty years ago, large fortress walls were installed between each of Drachen's three sections. The tunnels were closed out of fear that intruders might use them to infiltrate the city. All the passages that crossed from one sector to another were filled in. Presently, each district had its own independent subterranean channels.

In summary, the tunnels accessible from the nobles' district didn't extend beyond that city section's borders. None of the paths leading outside of Drachen remained.

"As I recall, there are only four entrances, one in each cardinal direction. If our intruder is down there, all we have to do is fortify the access points, and they'll be caught like a rat in a trap," Dante said.

"Precisely."

The reply came from one of the two responsible for kicking off this incident—Northheim's ninja, Sasuke.

"Sasuke!" Upon seeing the man, Forstner grabbed him by the collar. "What the hell do you have to say for yourself?!"

"There was an intruder in the nobles' district, so I moved to intercept. I didn't recognize her face or garb, but I suspect she's the rumored Seven Luminaries ninja."

"I didn't ask for a summary! I'm talking about how you took off without leave and started a fight on someone's house! As long as you're with Marquis Northheim, you answer to me, Gold Knight Forstner! Don't act on your own, especially not on your first damn day in the city!"

"My apologies. The intruder was unexpectedly swift. She might have reached the castle if I did not act when I did."

"I'm not interested in your excuses!"

Forstner was so enraged that he swung his fist and clocked Sasuke on the cheek.

The moment the punch landed...

"Ghhh!"

...Forstner's eyes went wide. It felt like he'd punched a boulder.

By contrast, Sasuke didn't even flinch. "If you wish to scold me, you can do it later," he stated. "For now, you must prioritize locking down those four entrances."

"You think you can order me around, on top of—?"

"All right, all right. Let's settle down," Dante interjected, stepping in between the two. After pacifying Forstner, he turned to Sasuke. "We found the tunnel entrance pried open, but that doesn't prove our rogue *kunoichi* is down there, you know. She might have done it to throw us off the trail, then hidden somewhere aboveground. Or perhaps she descended for a bit but has already come up through another entrance. Am I wrong?"

The points were sound. However, Sasuke shook his head. "That isn't possible."

"Why not?"

"Because ever since she went underground, I've been *tracking her footsteps and following her by ear.*"

"Excuse me?"

"The intruder moved deep into the tunnels, but she's made no attempt to return to the surface. She recognized my strength and realized I would capture her the moment she came back up. I imagine she'll stay down there to recuperate."

"Please, enough with the joking... You're claiming you can hear underground footsteps with all this noise? That's ridiculous."

"If I couldn't manage such a trivial thing, I never would have led the Special Forces."

"..."

Sasuke's feat was downright superhuman, yet he spoke of it so casually. Forstner's face paled. He was starting to think that maybe, just maybe, he was dealing with a genuine monster.

Dante had a different reaction. "Ha-ha-ha, how splendid. I should've expected nothing less from Yamato's famous rogue ninja. You do your rumors justice, Mr. Sasuke. It's truly inspiring to have you on our side. I'll have my men get to work guarding those entrances at once."

Dante called his troops over.

"H-hey, hold on!" Forstner stammered. "You really buy into this nonsense?!"

"Why wouldn't I?"

Forstner appeared even more bewildered, and a look of exasperation crossed Dante's face. "You really don't get it, do you?" he said before leaning in and whispering in Forstner's ear. "This fine gentleman has decided to stake his reputation on the intruder hiding beneath our feet. If she isn't there, he'll take all the blame. And if she is, we can hide that we acted on his advice and take all the credit. Either way, we leave with clean hands. Unless you'd rather have us spit apologies while inspecting the mansions of every noble in the district?"

Dante was a man who kept an eye out for opportunities. That's how he became a Gold Knight so young.

"...I guess you have a point."

Once Dante laid it all out, Forstner realized just how advantageous the situation was for them. They stood to lose nothing, and on top of that, he had no desire to go around waking a bunch of nobles in the dead of night to search their homes. Dante's proposal was perfectly agreeable.

"I'll have my men start at the west and south entrances and work their way in from there, so, Forstner, I'm counting on you and yours to do the same at the north and east entrances."

"Sure. We're on it."

Now all the imperial soldiers were on the same page regarding the search.

Once the higher-ups made their decision, Sasuke got ready as well. "In that case, I'll head belowground and—"

However...

"*You* are going to do nothing."

...Forstner drew his sword to put Sasuke in his place.

"Your job is to wait here on standby. A soldier who doesn't obey is useless to me. I want you to stay here with your head as empty as a fool's."

If Forstner accidentally allowed Sasuke to pull off something impressive, it would retroactively legitimize his earlier actions. No good would come to Forstner if he let that happen. If Sasuke joined him on the search, it could jeopardize the winning scenarios Dante explained.

"As you wish." Sasuke likely realized that to some extent. Instead of objecting, he merely took a step back.

"*Tch.* Move out, men!"

Even the ninja's obedience felt like he was flaunting his confidence. Forstner couldn't stand it. He clicked his tongue before mobilizing his soldiers.

All the while, Sasuke stood and watched, as ordered.

He couldn't care less who got the credit for his accomplishments. Glory was of little interest to him, and he saw no value in honor conferred. Others could praise him for his talents all they wanted, but if he wasn't satisfied with his performance, it all rang hollow. Sasuke desired those moments when he became fully cognizant of his own brilliance. That was where he found gratification and drive. It was narcissism of a kind. And because of it...

The old tunnels are simple passages of reinforced stone. Their straight and unadorned designs leave no places to hide. Anyone could find the intruder with enough people to throw at the job.

…he wasn't bothered.

Sasuke didn't concern himself with work others could handle. He was the one who'd noticed Shinobu's intrusion, intercepted her, and forced her into a situation where she had no choice but to trap herself in an underground dead end. He'd already done his part, and compared to his astounding feats, the grunt work about to take place was beneath him.

Forstner and Dante's plan elicited nothing from Sasuke, not even displeasure.

He had no reason to be upset.

The only thing that irked him…

"You know, you didn't need to make us go to all this trouble."

…was Shinobu's vain struggle.

In the deepest part of the old tunnels, there was a chamber that the city guard used as an armory. It was square, about thirty feet to a side, and packed full of wooden crates haphazardly stuffed with forgotten weapons and armor, or perhaps they'd just been deemed not worth the effort to retrieve.

Basically, the room was a scrap heap. And in that pile, hidden in the corner behind some of the crates, was a small living space comprising a bed and table. While living in Drachen as an exchange student, Shinobu had set up several such spots to use as bases of operation if things got hairy.

"Ow…!"

Shinobu's pained groans echoed through the cold, heavy air.

She was sitting on the bed and treating her wounds by lantern light.

"…Whew. Well, that should keep me on my feet for now."

She applied a medicinal ointment to dull the pain, then fixed it by winding a fabric bandage around her chest. That alone would go a long way toward keeping her mobile. It was a small mercy that none of her fractured ribs had punctured her organs or splintered.

"The situation's looking pretty gnarly, though."

Trapping herself here was a poor move. These underground channels were a dead end. Odds were, the imperial soldiers had already blocked off all four exits. She was caught.

However, there were no other options.

When I snuck down here, he probably tracked me by my footsteps…

Shinobu had little doubt of that.

After all, she could do that much, and although she disliked admitting it, her foe's ninja skills surpassed hers. Shinobu believed anything she could manage, Sasuke could, too.

If she took the tunnels to another exit to escape, he'd simply ambush her again. That was the best-case scenario, and with broken ribs slowing Shinobu down, the issue was that much more acute. Ultimately, the prodigy journalist elected to stay in the tunnels to treat her injuries, pull herself together, and give herself a fighting chance.

That was the logic behind fleeing to the dead end, anyway. But logic or not, hiding here was a bitter pill to swallow. It was a last resort, and it didn't do anything to fix the precariousness of her situation.

I can probably still get out, but it'd just be me…

Shinobu had set up more than a few secret bases during her exchange-student days. She'd also left *multiple* devices around Drachen. Setting them off would create enough chaos for her to escape.

Drachen's security would tighten as a result, though, making Masato and Roo's extraction more difficult.

Now that her original plan was in shambles, Shinobu had to grapple with a choice. She could give up on rescuing Masato and Roo and prioritize her own safe withdrawal, or she could hold fast to her mission and prioritize finding Masato and Roo. Between the two...

"Let's be real—there's no way I'm ditching Massy."

Her mind was made up.

She wasn't going to abandon them, not when she was the only person who could make the latter option a reality. It didn't matter how difficult it was going to be.

"Gosh, Shinobu, you're so compassionate," she said to herself. "And so courageous! It brings a tear to the eye."

The next issue was how to deal with the ninja.

Sasuke the Black Spider once headed up the Special Forces, and if Shinobu intended to complete her mission, then evading him wasn't an option. Even if she managed to sneak out of Drachen with Masato and Roo, running into a threat like Sasuke with people to protect was the absolute worst-case scenario. Thus, the only recourse was to defeat Sasuke first.

"I hope there's something in here I can use..."

To prepare for the upcoming rematch, Shinobu gathered the tools she'd stashed in her hideout and laid them out on the bed. There was a first aid kit, some wire, a few candles, a large bag of flour, some lantern oil, a hundred-odd feet of rope, alcohol, caltrops, some *kunai*, some grenades, flint, a hand-powered charger...

This pile had to coalesce into a plan that could turn this doomed predicament on its head.

Perhaps grenades could get the drop on Sasuke?

No. Shinobu had already used a flash-bang on him. Explosives would likely work on soldiers, but Sasuke was prepared for such weapons.

In that case, what if Shinobu poured oil everywhere and started a huge fire to incite panic?

Again, no. The soldiers were one thing, but Sasuke wasn't the type to be rattled, even with a blaze under his feet.

What if she just hid and waited for the guards to pass her?

Nope, that was the least realistic option. The old tunnels' construction and layout were very simple. There was nowhere to hide. As long as the imperials sent enough people to scour the place, they would find her. And even if she did manage to trick them somehow, there was no sneaking into the castle with that ninja alert aboveground.

No matter what Shinobu thought up, Sasuke's existence threw a wrench in it. She was powerless without a way to defeat him.

The problem was...

The guy's got no weaknesses.

"Rgh... Here they come..."

As if things weren't bad enough already, Shinobu's problems got more pressing. Footsteps sounded from somewhere above.

A wave of people approached from each of the four entrances.

Shinobu was in the deepest part of the tunnels, and she'd laid a fair number of booby traps on the path, but that would buy only so much time. In less than ten minutes, hostiles would pour into the abandoned armory.

Alarm rose within Shinobu, and she forced herself to take a deep breath. In times like this, staying calm was critical. There was no getting sloppy against these opponents.

"Y'know, maybe the calmest thing to do would be to bake some nice bread while I think my options over. Ha-ha, that'd sure be something."

Shinobu grabbed the big bag of flour, then gave her own bad joke a sarcastic laugh.

However...

"........."

...when she looked at the nearby candles, she was struck by a flash of inspiration.

That's it. I can use this to...

She'd figured out the one way to turn this desperate situation around.

It felt like divine revelation.

"Get in there, men! The intruder's one girl, and she's on her own! Ninja or not, if she's surrounded, we can get her! The first person who spots the *kunoichi* gets to help torture her!"

"Woo-hoo!"

"Heh-heh-heh! Where aaaare you? Where are you, little wench?"

"And remember, we want to be fast but thorough! I want that torchlight covering every inch of this place, top to bottom!"

The Drachen soldiers entered the old tunnels through every existing entrance, flooding in like water to an ant nest. They had every reason to believe that the intruder had fled down here, and they were determined to find her.

Midway through their search...

"Agh!"

...the one at the front of the line marching through the passage only wide enough to move single file let out a scream and sank down. Face twisted in pain, he shouted back, "Shit, that hurts! There's something on the ground!"

The others lowered their torches and discovered that the floor was covered in pointy metal bits.

"They're caltrops! Yamato ninja weapons!"

Forstner was farther back in the procession, and when he heard the news, his lips curled into a sneer. "If there are caltrops, then we're in the right place. Now we *know* she fled to the tunnels! Clear out those spikes! Our prey is close at hand!"

"Yes, sir!"

The soldiers did as ordered and swept the caltrops away with their swords. Before they could finish, Forstner impatiently charged forward...

"Just you wait! I'll be the one to claim the intruder's hea— GAH!"

...then tripped and fell ten feet beyond where the soldier had wounded his foot.

He landed on his rump as though he'd smacked into an invisible wall.

"S-Sir Forstner?!"

The Gold Knight scowled at the seemingly empty passage...

"String, hmm? A petty trick! Take—this?!"

...and swung his sword.

He was aiming for wires stretched across the tunnel at the height of the average adult's throat. Unfortunately, the cords were made of steel manufactured with techniques centuries ahead of this world's. Forstner's sword bounced off. The wires hung just as taut as before.

"Hrrrgh! Just crawl under them! If we don't hurry up, Heidekker's people are going to steal all the glory!"

Forstner was in a hurry, and the childish traps wasted his time. His expression twisted with annoyance, and as he barked orders to those at his back, he stooped down to pass beneath the steel cords.

However, that unstable posture proved to be his ruin.

"GAHHH!"

"Sir Forstner?!"

The Gold Knight slipped and smashed his face into the reinforced-stone floor.

"I-it's oil! The ground is covered in oil!"

"She must have set it up so you'd slip if you tried to crawl under the wire."

"What an obnoxiously simple setup..."

"DAAAAMN HERRRRRR!!!!"

Forstner roared furiously and beat the wall hard enough to leave a crack.

In that moment, his rage was all-consuming.

"...I won't let her get away with this. How dare she subject an esteemed Gold Knight to such humiliation?! That little bitch... Once we're done getting the intel we need from her, I'm going to torture her in every way I can think of until she breathes her last!"

Forstner and his troops were completely livid, and they surged down the tunnel like a tidal wave. They brute-forced their way through Shinobu's traps, trampled the wooden crates scattered about, hurled jars aside, smashed open barrels, and when they found sealed-off corridors, they cleared them out, too. They had no intention of letting Shinobu escape, and eventually, their diligent search led them to her base—the old storeroom in the deepest section of the complex.

"Come on out, you little whore!"

"Do try to watch your language. There's quite an echo down here, you know."

The exasperated comment came from Dante, who'd arrived at the storeroom just as Forstner did.

"Heidekker's man…! She wasn't on your side?!"

"She wasn't, and from your tone, I take it you were similarly unsuccessful. That said…" Dante swept his gaze across the abandoned armaments. "This is as deep as the tunnels go. If Sasuke was right about the intruder fleeing underground, this must be where she's hiding."

"Find her! Turn this place upside down and flush the rat out!"

""""Yes, sir!"""""

The dozens of soldiers violently searched the room. There was no finesse or technique to their inspection, merely raw force. They found everything hidden there, including a still-warm lantern, a bed, and a few ninja tools.

Then…

Up on the surface, Sasuke waited obediently for the search party to return. He wasn't idly standing there, either. To prevent the worst-case scenario, he paid close attention to all aboveground movement.

Nearly an hour after the teams left…

"Sasuke!"

…he heard the voice of his new superior, whom he'd met for the first time earlier that day.

Several dozen pairs of footsteps approached.

Forstner's team had completed the expedition.

Sasuke offered the group a respectful bow. "Welcome back. I trust you had no problems finding the intruder?"

"You CHEAP SWINDLER!"

The ninja didn't receive the affirmation he expected but the corpse of a brown rat. Forstner threw it at him.

"You sent us rummaging around in that den of traps, and all there was to find was a single damn rodent! The *kunoichi* wasn't there!"

"What do you have to say for yourself, Sasuke?"

As Forstner ranted and raved with his face bright red, Dante gave Sasuke a look that was far calmer but no less severe.

In reply...

"That can't be. Perhaps you missed her?"

...Sasuke remained confident of his judgment, instead casting doubt on the search.

Naturally, the two knights were indignant. "Shut your damn mouth!"

"Need I remind you that you were the one who assured us she was down there? This is on your head."

"..."

After menacingly reminding Sasuke that there would be consequences, Forstner and Dante set to discussing their next move.

Sasuke hadn't seen the tunnels for himself...

Impossible.

...and refused to question his call.

Nobody had more faith in Sasuke's talents than the man himself. He'd never mishear an opponent's footsteps; he was the Black Spider. Shinobu had definitely fled underground. That was a certainty, which meant she was still there. She had to be. However, the soldiers couldn't find her.

The only answer was a flaw in the sear—

＊　　＊　　＊

"""""_____?!?!"""""

That's when it happened.

A blast like thunder ripped through Drachen.

"Wh-wh-what was that?!"

"An explosion...?!"

It came from pretty close by.

While the imperial knights wondered what it could be...

"Messenger! Messenger, coming throooough!"

...a soldier wove his way over to them, his face pale.

"There was a blast of unknown origin at the second rampart separating the nobles' district from the commoners' district! It would appear that someone is trying to blow a hole in the wall!"

"Th-they're trying to what?!"

Given the situation, there was only one person who could be responsible.

"It's the *kunoichi*! So she was hiding aboveground after all!"

"She wants to destroy the wall so she can escape! We need to be there now! Move, move, move!"

"""""Yes, sir!"""""

The knights and soldiers rushed toward the scene of the explosion.

However...

"_____"

...Sasuke didn't follow.

That's strange.

As far as people in Drachen who might blast a hole in the wall, that *kunoichi* was the only possible culprit. She had the motive. However, it seemed like an odd play given the timing. Even if Forstner and Dante were right about her remaining topside this whole time, it would have been more practical to detonate the bomb while her pursuers were belowground. Waiting until they were on the surface offered no advantage.

Plus, the wall was designed to stop invaders from reaching the nobles' district from the commoner side, but not the other way around. There were stairs to climb on this side, and once at the top, getting down was just as easy. A conspicuous explosive seemed pointless.

No matter how you sliced it, Shinobu's actions were illogical. And that being the case, they were probably a diversion. By all accounts, the intruder was the same Seven Luminaries ninja who'd assisted the Blue Brigade, and it stood to reason that she possessed technology to set off bombs remotely.

Still, that doesn't tell me where she is!

Sasuke had called the soldiers' hunt into question, but when he thought about it, they'd probably done a fine-enough job. The old sector-crossing tunnels were blocked-off cul-de-sacs, and the soldiers flooded into every access point. Even incompetent imbeciles could have found someone hiding in such an uncomplicated structure.

Overlooking a gem or gold coin was one thing, but there was no meaningful cover to hide behind or complex terrain to take advantage of in the subterranean passages. Concealing a several-foot-tall living creature from dozens of eyes simply wasn't—

Wait, hold on.

Sasuke shuddered at the weight of his oversight.

There was nowhere to hide. That was a fact. However, that was only while considering the tunnels as they were ahead of the search. Things were different during.

The soldiers examined the passages and chambers by charging in with lots of backup, using only torches for light.

The question was, would they have noticed?

Would any of them perceive one more soldier among their ranks?

"Gah!"

Sasuke ground his teeth. He'd screwed up.

There were plenty of discarded suits of armor down there. Cobbling together a disguise must have been a simple thing. Even if the old equipment was a bit worn, it needed only to pass cursory glances hindered by dim lighting. Plus, there were troops from both Northheim's and Heidekker's forces down there. The two sides weren't close enough to visually identify a member of the other group from an impostor. A new addition would be quietly dismissed as a member of the opposite faction.

The tunnels lacked hiding places, but if Shinobu joined the soldiers, she could have escaped the search and marched with them right back to the surface!

It's okay. I can still make it!

Sasuke took off at a run.

There was no doubt in his mind that the intruder evaded the soldiers by blending in with them. However, that meant she returned to the surface at roughly the same time as Forstner and Dante. No matter how good her disguise, she couldn't have separated and gone in another direction without drawing suspicion, and she didn't seem the type to take that risk in a tunnel system with nowhere to run.

Once aboveground, she likely triggered the explosion somehow and drew all the knights and soldiers over to the wall. And there was only one reason she would do something like that: to create an opening to head the opposite way, toward the final wall between the nobles' district and the castle.

"_____!"

Confident in his assessment, Sasuke rushed to the wall surrounding the castle and threw open a service door meant for soldiers beside the main gate.

Inside...

"Going around you was never an option, y'see."

...was a heap of defeated soldiers. Standing in their center was the prodigy journalist Shinobu Sarutobi. The candles had been snuffed, bathing her in shadow.

The service door loudly slammed shut under its own weight, plunging the narrow passage for guards into deeper darkness.

However, the two *shinobi* met each other's gazes all the same.

Using their honed night vision, they tracked the other's movements down to finger twitches.

"You are a crafty one; I'll give you that," Sasuke said.

"That's what *shinobi* are all about, y'know."

"But in the end, it was for nothing. I have you now."

"You sure about that?"

Shinobu readied her *kunai* in the dark. Then...

"Honestly, I was planning on taking you out in the tunnels, so when you didn't come down and I lost track of your position, it gave me a pretty good scare. I worried what you'd do if you found me on my way here. But to my surprise, you're not quite as good as you're cracked up to be...*Mr. Sasuke.*"

...she gave the enemy a small sneer.

"A two-bit ninja like you would never notice my trap. I can take you down here, no problem."

Shinobu was baiting him. However, Sasuke was no greenhorn. It took more than that to get a rise from him.

If anything, he got more focused...

"Try me."

...and seized the initiative.

Sasuke fired off a series of long-range slashes with the wires he dual-wielded. The darkness was so heavy that the cords didn't even leave a visible arc, yet Shinobu evaded them.

She had the faintest of sounds of which to work off, the subtlest airflows, and her sixth sense, and by taking full advantage of them all, she survived. Some careful footwork allowed her to dodge most of the attacks, and she parried the rest with her *kunai.*

Sparks erupted where the weapons met. Sasuke was impressed by the brief glimpse he got of Shinobu's fearless expression. However...

Sure enough, her movements are dulled.

...her footwork was slower than it had been during their previous skirmish.

That gut shot he'd landed was paying dividends. It explained why Shinobu went through the soldiers' door instead of scaling the wall, too. Her wounds kept her from operating at peak capacity.

Sasuke pressed on, pushing Shinobu closer and closer to the wall...

She's finished!

...until she was left with nowhere to go. He swung his steel wire, fully intent on beheading her.

And that's when Shinobu made her play.

*   *   *

"Here, catch!"

"Wh—?!"

Moving with more speed and agility than she'd demonstrated during the fight, Shinobu snatched a burlap sack leaning against the wall and hurled it at Sasuke. His steel wires tore open the sack, causing its contents to spray in every direction.

Flour?! But why would she—?

"I was planning on taking you out in the tunnels."
"I worried what you'd do if you found me on my way here."
"A two-bit ninja like you would never notice my trap."

Sasuke recalled Shinobu's remarks from earlier.

A confined passage with minimal airflow, candles extinguished ahead of time, the huge amount of flour in the air, and Shinobu's *kunai.*

Oh no!

The chain of facts all came together in his head to form a single catastrophe. Ninjas took advantage of many phenomena to carry out their missions. Thus, Sasuke knew that a fire lit in a closed-off space full of fine particulate matter would lead to a massive explosion.

He was already in the middle of an attack.

The die was cast.

Sasuke's steel wire would collide with Shinobu's *kunai,* sending sparks flying.

There was no way to avoid it, no way to stop it.

*   *   *

"HRRRRRRRR!"

At least, there shouldn't have been.

However, Sasuke was a ninja who survived only on his skills. His ability to react to danger fell well outside of regular human bounds, and in emergencies, his body knew to take the best option available with no intervention from his brain necessary.

To avoid igniting the flour, he pulled his arm back on reflex.

For an instant, the combination of the power he put into his attack and the withdrawal exceeded the limits of his body. The burden of the opposed forces tore through the muscles in his arm.

Still, he got it done.

Sasuke wrenched his steel wire away from Shinobu, miraculously foiling her scheme.

And his choice to do so...

"Yup. I knew you'd try that."

...was the blunder that spelled the end of the duel.

A dust explosion was caused by lighting a fire in an airtight or low-circulation enclosure full of fine particles. This triggered a process that led to rapid air combustion. The phenomenon was incredibly dangerous, and it was why coal mines and flour mills prohibited fires of any kind.

That said...

"Even starting a flame doesn't guarantee a dust explosion. Not by a long shot."

…the conditions were surprisingly strict.

One could happen to the unfortunate, but scattering some flour and lighting a fire wasn't going to do much most times. Certain places banned open flames to prevent rare worst-case scenarios.

Shinobu pinning her survival on something that unlikely was foolish.

"But at the same time, you never know who'll hit that one-in-a-million catastrophe."

The slim possibility carried a surprising amount of weight.

Suppose there was a nuclear warhead with a 10 percent chance of actually detonating. Would the crappy nuke's unreliable nature prevent it from changing the world? Obviously not. Even at one-in-ten odds, the mere fact that it had the *potential* to cause devastation meant it had the same deterring effect as a top-shelf bomb that exploded every time.

A faulty nuke could change the world, and that was because people refused to gamble when ruin was a possibility, even if the probability was low.

Shinobu had quite literally felt Sasuke's talent in her bones. Even in this world, millers knew about dust explosions, and there was no way that a ninja like him, a *killer* like him, would be ignorant of them. Ninjas took advantage of many phenomena to carry out their missions, after all.

Shinobu trusted he'd catch on to the potential danger because he was talented. And upon realizing the threat, Sasuke would naturally try to skirt doom because he was talented. And because he was talented, he would succeed.

Despite lacking time to consciously respond, his reflexes had seized control, reacting in a way no normal person could have.

And that movement *created* something.

It provided a moment when that unassailably capable ninja was vulnerable.

"We're in a building full of flour with poor airflow, and you were about to make a spark. The odds of an explosion were low, but with talent like yours, *there was a one hundred percent chance you would respond in time to avoid that one-in-a-million disaster.* All I had to do was use that to take you down."

"I...see..."

Sasuke was strung along to this fatal moment.

Shinobu's *thrown kunai* came lancing for him, and he had no way to dodge. When he felt it sink into his throat, he knew that death would soon take him.

Sasuke the Black Spider wanted to become the greatest *shinobi.* He'd put everything he had to that end, and he'd trained for any crisis that came his way. His aim was to elevate his very being into a form of art.

But it backfired.

Sasuke was more skilled than Shinobu, more skilled than anyone. *And that was why her plan succeeded.*

"I suppose that's that...isn't it?"

Dying this way had a sort of karmic irony to it. And Sasuke, a man who'd spent his life pursuing self-improvement at the expense of all else, found it strangely satisfying.

Rather than offer any futile resistance, he gave in to the fatigue of death and collapsed to his knees.

Then...

"I miscalculated. You, ma'am, are a far greater ninja than I gave you credit for."

...he offered the victor his praise, along with the first genuine smile he'd shown her.

In all likelihood, not even Sasuke recalled the last time he'd grinned so sincerely.

Shinobu responded with an impish grin...

"You miscalculated, yeah, but your new answer's wrong, too."

...then pulled her "press" armband from within her skirt...

"I'm no ninja; I'm a prodigy journalist, thank you very much."

...and proudly wrapped it around her arm for display.

She received no reply.

The mighty foe who blocked her path had already breathed his last...

"Still, I'll take heart knowing I was good enough to earn a compliment from such a capable guy."

...and Shinobu paid respects to his corpse.

She abandoned the ninja path halfway along, but this man kept on it. Shinobu had nothing but respect for Sasuke for that.

⚔ The Measure of Masato Sanada ⚔

The Tidal Breath war magic blasted the orbital military satellite to smithereens.

Before Neuro closed the magical gate, he tilted the pillar of water so it would collapse directly upon the battle between Yamato and Freyjagard. His aim was to use the leftover potential energy to crush both the sides and the High School Prodigies. The massive tower became a sword that could cleave the stars themselves, cutting through the air as it crashed toward the ground. It was nearly two hundred feet in diameter, and it was impossible to guess at the volume of water contained within. If it connected, the deluge would flatten the entire battlefield and wash everything away.

However...

...the Prodigies knew about the terrible power of war magic. And knowing that Neuro would turn hostile also meant understanding he wouldn't honor their old treaty. In a sense, the Prodigies saw this coming. So naturally, they'd prepared a counter.

A moment later, a star burst into being in the night sky.

*　　*　　*

The new sun burned bright enough to turn the black sky white, and its radiance, along with tremendous heat, devoured the star-rending blade.

A few beats after the explosive flash, a terrible wind pounded the earth. It was as though a natural disaster had occurred from nowhere, and the two armies screamed in confused terror.

However...

...the High School Prodigies were unshaken.

They were the ones who caused the blast.

Tsukasa, Ringo, and Bearabbit reviewed the results from within the swaying helicopter.

"That's a direct high-altitude hit fur Thor's Hammer."

"How are we on radiation?"

"No worries. Our pawsition is well outside the area of effect."

"Then it sounds like we're good on all fronts."

The incredible flash that had sent the fight into chaos was the explosion from a nuclear missile fired to counteract Tidal Breath.

Just as Neuro's side had a trump card in the form of war magic, the Prodigies had their own in the form of nuclear arms. Naturally, they'd developed a robust-enough firing system that losing one satellite wasn't enough to ruin things. As soon as Bearabbit recognized that the towering blade of water erupting from Drachen was falling toward Yamato, he fired the red emergency flares that signaled a necessary nuke launch. When the watchtower stationed on the Elm border spotted the flares, the Bearabbit AI installed in its observation terminal issued the order to the missile site via the wireless network of public broadcasting obelisks scattered throughout Elm.

That triggered the launch of the Thor's Hammer missile.

Instead of relying on the satellite, a Bearabbit AI loaded directly onto the missile guided it to the target. When the Thor's Hammer exploded at high altitude, it did so with enough destructive power to blast the aquatic sword to bits.

Ringo let out a huge sigh. "Phew... I'm so glad...it all worked out..."

"Were you worried?"

"I-it's just...I couldn't stop thinking...about what would happen...if it didn't..."

A missile intercept without satellite guidance was a method reserved for emergencies. Tsukasa and Ringo would have been fine. The helicopter was quick enough to dodge Neuro's attack if it moved at top speed. The same was true for Aoi and Shura below. However, the slightest malfunction or delay between the Bearabbit AIs would've meant death for everyone else.

The mere idea of the possible death toll was frightening.

Despite Ringo's worries...

"I was as calm as could be the whole time. That anti-war magic defense system was developed by the smartest person I know, and I was sure it wouldn't be so easily foiled."

...Tsukasa was fully confident in her countermeasures.

The nuclear missile–based anti-war magic air defense network was designed to prevent a repeat of tragedy in Dormundt. Ringo, Earth's greatest scientific mind, would never let the Prodigies' enemies carry out evil like that twice.

Now that the system had successfully thwarted the attack, it shifted to its other mode—*offense*.

There was more than one Thor's Hammer missile.

"Should we retailiate?"

Including the one just used, Tsukasa and the others had a full dozen Thor's Hammers stationed at various locations around

Elm. The Prodigies were the ones who'd proposed the treaty forbidding the use of war magic, so they'd avoided using any nukes preemptively. However, they now had the pretense of retribution. The Prodigies' side in the war faced a tremendous numbers disadvantage. Between the army they faced now, the greater one to come, and the enemy's stronghold of Drachen, there were plenty of juicy targets.

However...

"No, let's hold back."

...Tsukasa elected not to play that card.

Retaliatory strikes were a powerful tool in a war between two states. The more devastating the attack, the less willing the enemy would be to make their next military action. Here, though, Neuro was misappropriating the nation of Freyjagard for his own ends. He'd started the war to further his personal ambitions, and he didn't care how much damage the country suffered. Neuro's attack proved he was willing to kill many of his own troops if it meant the Prodigies went with them.

"The lives of others simply don't factor into his calculations. Hitting back against a foe like that would expend us for little gain."

Ultimately, their enemy was Neuro and Neuro alone. Unless they could pin down his exact position, blindly firing off Thor's Hammers would cause a senseless loss of life with nothing to show for it. That hardly seemed like a winning strategy.

"Besides, Masato's still in Drachen, and I imagine Shinobu's made her way into the city by now, too."

"But if we don't strike fur into him, isn't there a possibility he'll use that same war magic again?"

"I wouldn't worry about that," Tsukasa replied confidently. It wasn't empty bravado, either. "Were Neuro capable of firing that off easily, he never would've bothered making peace with us in the first place."

Based on Neuro's actions and the way he negotiated, Tsukasa more or less understood what the man was capable of. Discerning that much was where Tsukasa Mikogami excelled. He wasn't in the business of misreading foes or falling for their bluffs and threats.

"That war magic undoubtedly cost him a lot. That's why he aimed for our satellite instead of just attacking us directly."

Tsukasa conceded that it was a savvy move. Neuro could have launched his war magic directly at the Prodigies, but if the satellite was still running, they would have spotted the attack before it landed. Plus, on a purely geographic level, the myriad mountain ranges between Drachen and Yamato would've prevented Neuro from getting a clean shot. Any time between Neuro starting his spell and it landing would've given Ringo the chance to use the helicopter, and Aoi her physical prowess, to escape. Neuro had mobilized his army under the pretext of revenge for Yamato overthrowing the dominion government, but the only thing he and the other grandmasters actually cared about was killing the Seven Heroes—the High School Prodigies who stood in the way of resurrecting Father. No matter how many Yamato soldiers Neuro slaughtered with his war magic, it wouldn't mean a thing if the Prodigies escaped alive.

Neuro was keenly aware of where his interests lay. That's why he chose the method guaranteed to chip away at the Prodigies' resources, rather than risk an all-or-nothing attack.

In other words...

"Our opponent is taking this just as seriously as we are."

Ringo had the skills to build a new satellite, but she was in Yamato and lacked Elm's resources and facilities. Solving this new issue would take time, and Neuro would definitely seize upon that. He was liable to send in troops, even if they weren't prepared yet.

If the Prodigies hoped to win this war, they'd need to overcome this major impediment to their communication and reconnaissance capabilities. Losing the satellite in the war's opening moments was a serious setback.

"For now, let's focus on regaining control of the situation on the ground. We can worry about the future later," Tsukasa said, turning his gaze downward.

Below, the battlefield that had been so alive with shouts and screams moments ago was deathly quiet. That battle wasn't over, but nobody's heart was in it anymore. Humans weren't built to process so many incomprehensible events in rapid sequence, and the imperial and Yamato soldiers were beyond the breaking point.

This was bad.

Until now, the Yamato forces had kept their focus razor-sharp, whereas the imperials were in a panic because of the surprise attack. That's why things went so well for the Prodigies' side, despite the massive numbers disadvantage. Now...both sides were on even emotional footing. If they kept fighting mindlessly as they were, the huge troop discrepancy would spell Yamato's defeat.

Tsukasa felt the change in the air and quickly made the call to pull out. "We haven't done enough damage to properly set the stage for our future battles yet, but there's no helping it. Bearabbit, send the evacuation order."

"With the rendezvous pawsition you set in the briefing?"

"That's right. We'll follow the original plan and fall back to Mt. Sou'unzan, then make it our first line of defense and prepare for the coming imperial attack. There's nothing more we can do tonight."

The evacuation order echoed out loud from the helicopter's megaphone over the silent, dispirited battlefield. At the announcement, the Yamato soldiers began fleeing in unison. The imperial army couldn't muster the energy or willpower to pursue, so the samurai escaped quickly.

Thanks to a successful surprise attack, the first clash in the empire's attempt to retake Yamato ended in victory for the Yamato side. However, it was really a triumph only when considered in a vacuum. The Prodigies had lost Ringo's military satellite and one of their Thor's Hammers. Furthermore, they'd been forced to retreat with much of the imperial vanguard still alive. Tsukasa knew how heavy a shackle around their legs those two facts would become later.

The next day, the second imperial corps arrived at the border, numbering fifty thousand strong.

After joining up with the first imperial corps for a total of nearly eighty thousand, the war on Yamato began in earnest.

Just before Ringo's missile intercept…

"What…is that thing…?"

…Shinobu was on top of the castle ramparts in the heart of the imperial capital. From her perch, she had a front-row seat to the raging pillar—the war magic Tidal Breath—surging from the military headquarters in the nobles' district.

"Urk…"

Faced with the staggering magnitude of its power, Shinobu found herself breathless. In that moment, she was faced with a realization: The opponent she and her friends were up against was just as dangerous as they'd feared.

That meant it was all the more critical their group reunited and returned to full strength quickly. All the Prodigies needed to be together so they could fight as a team, and for that to happen, Shinobu had to find Masato Sanada.

With that thought at the forefront of her mind, Shinobu prepared to leap from the rampart walkway to the courtyard below. Before she got the chance, though...

"Wait, Shinobu...?!"

...she heard a voice beside her.

It was a familiar one. As a matter of fact, it belonged to the very guy she was thinking of.

She turned...

"What are you doing here, Shinobu?"

...and saw Masato Sanada standing at the entrance to the rampart walkway, eyes wide in surprise.

Shinobu's heart soared, and she rushed over and grabbed him by the hand. "Massy!"

She'd known he was nearby, but it was truly fortunate to run into him so quickly.

"Where's Roo? Is she not with you?" Shinobu asked.

"Li'l Roo? She's not here right now. She's off on her *first big errand*."

"That's a shame, but oh well. I'll pick her up later, so for now, we should—"

"Whoa, whoa, whoa, whoa! Back up a sec!"

Shinobu tried to blaze through the conversation, but Masato stepped on the brakes. He forcibly pulled his hand free of Shinobu's. "Don't go tryin' to move the discussion along before you've got a consensus. First off, what the hell do you think you're doin' here? And more importantly..." His expression turned sour. "What the *fuck* are you guys playing at, going to war with Neuro?"

There was faint rage on his face. Neuro was the Prodigies' ticket back to Earth, and unsurprisingly, Masato was angry that Tsukasa and the others had taken hostile action against him.

However...

"I made myself crystal goddamn clear. *Don't do anything dumb.* So what's the big idea?"

"Would you still feel that way if I told you that Neuro's goal involves killing Lyrule?"

"...What?"

...Masato wasn't present in Yamato, so he couldn't be blamed for not knowing that the situation had changed. The powers at work that affected the seven teenagers from Earth and the world at large were a half-finished jigsaw puzzle before. The Prodigies weren't working with the full picture. Now, the missing pieces were clear. Siding with Neuro was a *viable choice* when Masato left, but now, that option was worthless.

"We traced the Seven Luminaries' roots to the ruins of an elf village deep in the forests of Yamato. That's where we met...her, the person who brought us over to this world. And she told us everything."

Shinobu relayed the story to Masato.

She told him about how the evil dragon was actually a mage from another world named Father and that Yggdra—the one who summoned them—and Neuro were both homunculi Father had created. Then she spoke about the invasion and subsequent war a thousand years ago that shaped this planet's history. She explained the magical seal that ended the conflict and the elves who passed it through their lineage for centuries. Lastly, she revealed that Neuro and the other reincarnated homunculi were plotting to kill Lyrule to bring about Father's return.

The Prodigies saw and learned a lot in that village, and Shinobu was careful not to leave anything out.

"…You know that sounds like something out of a video game, right?" Masato replied.

"C'mon, you already knew that our world wasn't the only one out there. I think it's a little late to be surprised."

Truthfully, Shinobu was a bit skeptical about the magical seal and world domination stuff, too. No matter Neuro's motives, though, the fact that he sought to murder a friend meant cooperating with him was out of the question. The Prodigies owed their lives to Lyrule; surely they all agreed they had to side with her.

"Look, we need to get the hell out of Drachen. It'd be a huge problem if Neuro took you prisoner. You understand, right? Now, come—"

Shinobu reached for Masato's arm again. Swiftness was of the essence. But then…

…there came a shot.

"Huh?"

A wave of agony lanced through Shinobu. It was so intense that it completely overwrote the pain from her broken ribs. Fire burned her from the inside.

The source was a small smoking gun clenched in Masato Sanada's hand.

"You asked if I still feel the same way? Yeah, I do."

"Mas…sy?"

"It sucks having to sacrifice Lyrule, but my employees' futures matter way more."

"Ah!"

As a prodigy journalist, Shinobu was an expert at reading

©Sacraneco

people, and she could tell there was no affection in Masato's voice or expression.

"Unlike Tsukasa, I don't believe in people.

"*Aside from one exception*, I only trust my talent.

"Since day one, it's been my policy to handle everything. I haven't made my guys shoulder any burdens.

"So…they're doomed without me."

Masato had restored the Sanada Group by attending every administrative meeting of every one of the enterprise's subsidiaries, issuing orders directly. He was the complete opposite of Tsukasa, who recognized his own imperfections and chose to rely on the talents of others. For Masato, his decisions were absolute, and he ran his businesses as a one-man monarchy.

Would people reared in that sort of business environment be able to step up and take his place while he was gone?

Not a chance.

Masato wasn't like Tsukasa, who planned for every contingency up to and including his own disappearance when building his organizations. For Masato, no one could run his companies but him.

He didn't foster his people's development. On the contrary, he robbed them of opportunities to grow. This allowed him to rule them. He chose that path.

"I control everything, so I've got a duty to handle it all alone for them."

He didn't waver. He *couldn't*. Because that was who Masato Sanada was—a prodigy businessman.

That's why Masato separated from the group and staked his wager on Neuro. He'd already made his choice. He'd told the others about it when he left them.

"Why the hell'd you have to come, Shinobu? Now that I know you're here...

"...I can't let you leave!"

"..."

Another gunshot, and Shinobu's body collapsed.

Shortly after Masato shot Shinobu with a vertical two-barrel flint-lock pistol fresh from the imperial workshops, a couple of members of his Lakan mercenary team, the Qinglong Gang, rushed over.

"Are you okay, Chancellor Advisor?!"

"We heard gunfire!"

"I'm fine," Masato replied. "That was me. Nothin' to worry about."

"Who's the chick?"

"...An old teammate."

Masato stowed his gun in its holster, then turned to one particularly brawny mercenary who came with the others. "Are you and your men all ready, Captain?"

"Of course. *'Be quick, be strong, charge lots'* is our motto, ain't it?"

The creed had changed since the last time Masato heard it, but he was in no mood to jokingly call attention to that. His expression remained grim as he muttered, "Good."

Then he gave the order.

"Send word to all members of the Qinglong Gang. As per Neuro's instructions, we're leaving Drachen...

"...and setting out for the Republic of Elm."

AFTERWORD

THERE'S GONNA BE AN ANIME ADAPTATIOOOOOOOOO
OOOOOOOOOOOOOOOOOOOOOOOOOOOOOOOOOOOOOO
OOOOOOOOOOOOOOON!!!

On that note, thank you all for buying and reading Volume 8.
I'm Riku Misora, the author.

You probably saw it written on the *obi*. It's true—there's going
to be an anime adaptation! This never would have been possible
without your steadfast support.

There will be plenty of news about the anime in the coming
days, and I'll be sure to post about it on my Twitter account whenever information drops. I'd love it if you gave me a follow.

Let's all look forward to the anime adaptation together!

As far as the novels go, this book marks the beginning of the
final chapter of the High School Prodigies' story. The full picture
of what's going on is finally clear, and the Prodigies have identified what their role as the Seven Heroes actually means. With the
endgame in sight, they're going to do whatever it takes to get there.

And when they do, Tsukasa will be forced to confront that prophecy Gustav left him.

I hope you'll continue following the seven High School Prodigies in an unfamiliar world for a little longer.

Now, I have some people I'd like to thank for helping make this book a reality.

Sacraneco, your illustrations are…amazing. I don't know how to put it except *"amazing"* (I say, breaking into a nosebleed). In particular, that Shinobu on the cover is mega cute! I can't get enough of those thighs and the way you can see the shadow of her boobs. I mean, meow!

Then there's Kotaro Yamada, who's working on the manga adaptation. The story has finally reached the currency summit, which is the prelude to the Yamato arc (the election arc). Reading the new chapters is always a highlight for me.

Next, I'd like to thank everyone over at the GA Bunko editorial department for carrying the series all the way to getting an anime adaptation.

And finally, once again, my utmost gratitude to the readers for supporting this series for so long.

I hope we meet again in Volume 9.